The END of the RAINBOW

Filled with excitement, Megan pulled herself away from Tom and ran forwards, her arms outstretched. But she had forgotten the ice. The next moment, she slipped and fell with a little scream of pain.

People nearby gathered round immediately, and Tom pushed through the crowd and bent over her anxiously. She was already trying to get up, but her leg was twisted beneath her and she sank back with a little moan of pain and gazed at him beseechingly.

"Grandma – find Grandma for me, Tom. Don't let her disappear."

He glanced over to the booth where Megan had seen the man and woman, but they had vanished. He couldn't follow without leaving Megan alone on the ice. He bent over her again.

"Where does it hurt, Meggie? What have you done?"

"It's just my ankle – I've twisted it, that's all." She tried to get up again but the pain showed in her face. "Please, Tom, go after Grandma."

"I can't, Meggie. She's already gone. I'd never find them now, in the dark and all this crowd. And I can't leave you here."

Also available in the Forget Me Not series:

Forget me Not

The END of the RAINBOW

Donna Baker

SCHOLASTIC

Scholastic Children's Books
Commonwealth House,
1–19 New Oxford Street,
London WC1A 1NU, UK
A division of Scholastic Ltd
London ~ New York ~ Toronto ~ Sydney ~ Auckland

First published by Scholastic Ltd, 1998

Copyright © Donna Baker, 1998

ISBN 0 590 13943 6

Typeset by TW Typesetting, Midsomer Norton, Somerset
Printed by Caledonian International Book Manufacturing Ltd, Glasgow

10 9 8 7 6 5 4 3 2 1

Prologue

The memory haunted her dreams for months afterwards.

It was in the year 1860, soon after Megan Price's sixteenth birthday. The iron skip, hauled to the surface of the mine by the horse that plodded patiently, endlessly, in circles at the top of the shaft. She and the other pit-bank wenches, reaching out to unhook it and empty out the coals. The sudden fumble, or stumble – nobody was ever quite sure what had happened – and the screams as the skip swayed, tipped and shed its black, knobbly cargo back into the depths.

The yells of terror far below, as the coal rattled against the sides of the shaft and shattered on the pit floor. The silence...

Megan woke with a jump and stared wildly around the tiny room. Daylight was beginning to filter through the bit of old sacking hung across the small, cracked window. Her two younger sisters were still asleep, breathing evenly on the tumble of rags that served them all for a bed. In the corner, behind the tattered cloth that had been rigged up as a curtain, her brother Emlyn snored in the bed he shared with

1

Owen, with little Dafydd snuffling beside him.

It had been a dream. *The* dream. The dream in which she lived it all again. And woke to the knowledge that it was real.

It really had happened. The skip, tilting sideways. The coal, pouring out and down the shaft. The terrible cries. The silence.

The bodies, brought out in another skip, with men waiting for it this time where the pit-bank wenches usually stood. The bodies, crushed and blackened.

The body of her own father.

Chapter 1

"You can't marry again." Megan stared at her mother. "Dadda's only been dead three months. You can't have forgotten him already."

Dilys Price sighed with exasperation. "It's not a question of forgetting, *bach*. I've got a family to raise, haven't I? There's only you and Owen bringing in any wages, and little enough they are. How d'you think I'm going to feed the little ones?"

"And how much is Morgan Jones going to help?" Megan demanded. "He spends all his time down the tavern. Dadda would turn in his grave if you married him."

"Your dad'll do no turning in his grave, or anywhere else," Dilys retorted. "He'll be too glad of a good rest. I tell you, Meg, he's in the best place. I only wish I could be there with him. There's no pleasures in this life for such as us. We just have to struggle through, and that's what I'm doing. And if Morgan Jones is willing to give me a helping hand, I'll take it and be glad of it."

"A helping hand? Morgan Jones doesn't know what that is! It's you who'll be doing the helping – waiting on him hand and foot." Megan stared at her mother. "Can't you see, Mam? Don't you realize it?"

Dilys turned away.

"No, I don't see. All I know is there's not enough money coming into the house to feed all the mouths in it. Four little ones under five – how am I supposed to manage on what you and our Owen earn, and the few bits of stuff I can do at home? It'll be another year before Emlyn can go into the pit, and there'll still be three of 'em left. I don't have any choice, Meg, see?"

Megan gazed at her, feeling helpless. Her mother was right. Owen's money from the pit and her own from working as a pit-bank wench could not keep seven of them. But Morgan Jones...

Megan had never liked Morgan. He lodged in a room at the other end of the row of hovels and she had always hated passing his door, fearful that he would come out and catch her. There was something in his small, mean eyes that scared her, something in the way he looked at her.

"Can't you send a letter to Grandma?" she asked. "Surely she'd help. I mean, if she knew..."

But Dilys's mouth hardened. "I got the minister to write when your dad died. She never even answered. Too high and mighty in London to bother about her own son! But she did all right for herself when she married, look, so why shouldn't I?"

"Grandma didn't marry Morgan Jones," Megan retorted, but Dilys had gone out to the scullery and was crashing their few cooking pans together.

It was time for Megan to go to the pit. She threw her shawl around her shoulders, thrust her feet into her clogs and went out into the cobbled street. The sky was obscured by the smoke from the forges, and the air was full of its acrid tang. The clatter of pit machinery, which went on day and night, filled her ears.

Morgan Jones! She glanced at the house where he lived as she hurried past and caught a glimpse of his face, staring out through the grimy window. He saw her and grinned.

I can't live in the same house with him, she thought. I can't.

Chapter 2

Megan had worked at the mine since she was seven years old. She had never been underground like Owen, who had started at the same age, going down the pit with a basket to gather loose coal from holes at the sides of the tunnels. Megan had always been at the top, helping unload the skips or pick up fallen lumps. She had never known a day when her face, hands and clothing had not been blackened by coal-dust.

Owen was thirteen now, and worked as a hurrier on the carts, pushing them along the narrow tracks. He started work at four in the morning and stayed down the pit until gone five in the afternoon. He worked half-naked, for it was hot down below and the work was hard. He was already developing a stoop from the constant bending in the low tunnels, and he didn't seem to have grown much lately.

There had been other babies in the Price family, but most of them had died. Some hadn't even got as far as being born. The little ones, Emlyn, Dafydd, Bronwen and Gwen, were often poorly, and Gwen had rickets and couldn't walk yet. But they would all have to go to work when they reached the age of six or seven, no

matter how frail they were.

Meanwhile, Dilys Price had to stay at home to look after them. You could take one little one to the mine or a factory and sit them in a corner, but not four. She earned what she could at home from trouser-finishing for a tailor in Merthyr Tydfil. Each week she would collect the unfinished garments and buy the trimmings she needed — black, red and white cottons, thread, soap, gimp and twist. She then worked as many hours of the day or night as she had to in order to finish the work for the next week. Sometimes she sat up until past midnight, working by the light of a candle stump, and then got up at four to see Owen and Megan off to the mine.

Megan knew how hard her mother worked. She knew that even this only brought in a few shillings a week. Sometimes there was no work at all, and then Dilys would look for some cleaning to do, or take in washing. But there weren't many people in the Welsh valleys who could afford to pay for their washing to be done.

It wasn't surprising that her mother should look for another man to help with the expenses. But did she have to marry him? And did it have to be Morgan Jones?

"Why don't you take a lodger?" she asked, and Dilys snorted.

"And where would he sleep? Tell me that! We've only got two rooms, and there's four of you in the back one. We'll have to share with the little ones as it is."

There was no more to be said. And one morning a few weeks later, Dilys went off to the church and came back as Mrs Jones.

Morgan came with her. He grinned at Megan and put his arm round her. She felt a creeping horror and wanted to pull away, but for her mother's sake she gave him a wavery smile and stayed where she was.

"So you're my little girl now!" Morgan Jones said. "Well, I've always wanted a little girl like you. Pretty little thing. We'll get along just fine, won't we?"

Megan saw the other children look at him dubiously. Owen had gone to the mine. He hadn't said much but she knew he disliked Morgan Jones as much as she did, and meant to keep out of the house as much as possible. Megan wished she could do the same. But her mother still needed her help with the children.

Morgan Jones let her go and took Dilys up the road to the Miner's Arms to celebrate. There was a pile of trousers to be finished, but he didn't seem to have noticed them. He'll notice all right when the money doesn't come in at the end of the week, Megan thought. And when is he going to go to work himself?

But she didn't have time to worry about that. She'd been given a couple of hours off for her mother's wedding but now she had to hurry to the mine. She left Emlyn in charge of the others until Dilys came back and ran up the street, her clogs splashing in the coal-black mud.

*   *   *

Morgan Jones didn't go to work. He said he had a bad back so he stayed in bed late in the mornings and spent his days in the Miner's Arms. When Megan came home a few evenings later he was sitting in the rickety armchair her father had used, watching her mother sew trousers. The little children were huddled on an old mattress in a corner. Owen was on a stool, eating a bowl of potatoes and staring sullenly at the tiny fire.

"There you are, Meg." Dilys was looking nervous. "Waiting for you, I've been. I got something to tell you."

"What?" It couldn't be anything good. Everyone looked so miserable.

"Your father's lost his job," Dilys said baldly. "His back's too bad to go down the mine any more and they won't take him on above ground."

"They've got it in for me, see," Morgan said. "The foreman's always had a down on me." He glanced at Megan, his eyes not quite meeting hers. "Been trying to get rid of me for months, he has."

I'm not surprised, Megan thought. "So what are you going to do?" she asked. "Look for another job?"

"Well, there isn't much point to that, now, is there? I mean, if I can't work, I can't work. It's a proper shame – I was hoping to make things a bit better for you all, see. But as it is…" He looked away, into the fire.

"As it is," Megan said, "we're going to have to make things better for you, aren't we?"

His small eyes swivelled back to stare at her. "And what is that supposed to mean?"

"Well, you've got a family now, haven't you? We can work to keep you. Our Owen and me can do longer hours at the mine, our Emlyn's old enough to start gathering coal, you could even send little Gwen down to learn hurrying. I daresay she could earn a few shillings before she pegs out—"

"*Megan!*"

"Well, isn't that what he wants?" she demanded, facing her mother. "Isn't it what he wanted all along? He never meant to work for us. He wanted to move in here and let us work to keep him, that's what he wanted. And now he's got it."

"Megan, you mustn't talk about your father like that—"

"He's *not* my father!" Megan shouted. "My father's dead, don't you remember? Down the mine, he died, working to help keep us all. And now you've brought this – this *scrounger* into the house for us to keep. What are we supposed to do? What are *you* going to do? We work all the hours God sends as it is. How are you going to feed us all, with *him* sitting there on his fat backside doing nothing but eat and spend money in the Miner's Arms? Oh Mam," she cried, suddenly breaking into tears, "why did you have to do it? Why did you have to marry him?"

She sat down on a stool, burying her head in her arms. Dilys moved to lay her hand on Megan's shoulder but Morgan glowered at her and she drew back. Owen finished his potatoes and put down the bowl. The little ones drew closer on their mattress, staring with wide, frightened eyes.

"I'll not have it," Morgan said harshly. "I'll not have impertinence from a bit of a girl in my own house. You'll make her say sorry, Dil, or out she goes."

Megan lifted her head and stared at him. Her mother was white-faced.

"Morgan! You can't mean that. I can't turn her out – not my own daughter—"

"I've told you, I'll not have her cheeking me. You heard the things she called me. D'you expect me to sit here in my own chair, in my own house, and listen to that sort of cheek from a hussy—"

"*Your* chair? *Your* house?" Megan flared. "That's my *father's* chair you're sitting on, and this is *our* house. You haven't paid a penny towards *anything* since you came here." She looked at Owen's bowl. "We've always been poor, but our Owen would have had more than a few potatoes to eat after a day's work. That's all there is because we're having to feed *you* as well now, and there just isn't enough to go round."

"So maybe you'd better go and do a few more hours' work," Morgan growled. "That'll bring in some more money, and get you out of my way into the bargain." He turned to his wife. "I tell you, Dil, if she don't mend her ways there's going to be real trouble in this house."

"She didn't mean it," Dilys quavered. "She didn't really mean it – did you, Meg? Say you're sorry, there's a good girl. You can see you've upset your father."

Megan stared at her. Sorry? she thought. But I'm not sorry. I meant every word of it. It's true. Why should I say I'm sorry?

She saw the white, worn face, the trembling lips. She saw the thin body, the fingers sore from too much sewing. She thought of the children, too young yet to work, slowly starving. And the ones who had died, the babies who had never been born.

"All right, I'm sorry," she mumbled, feeling as if she were selling her soul. She went to the table and poured herself a cup of water. There was a hunk of bread there too and she hacked a piece off and began to eat.

Morgan Jones was watching her. She could feel his small eyes on her back.

How could she go on living here, with him? But what else was there for her to do?

Chapter 3

"Where's Mam?" Megan asked. She had come home from work to find the house empty except for Morgan Jones. He was sitting as usual in the old armchair and he had stoked up the fire.

"Gone to the tailor to see if there's any more work for her. He left her a bit short this week."

Suddenly, all the misery of the past months welled up inside her. Dadda's death, the struggle to manage without his wage, her mother's decision to marry this man who crouched like a great spider in the corner, day in, day out, week after week, clawing at everything that was brought into the house... She couldn't watch her words any longer.

"You mean *you've* left her short. You spent all her money in the Miner's Arms."

Morgan's face darkened. "I've told you before, Megan, I'll not stand any cheek from you—"

"No, what you don't want is the *truth*. It's not cheek when it's true." She faced him. "I've bitten my tongue with you because I didn't want to upset Mam. But now she's not here so I can say what I like." She took a deep breath. "It was the biggest mistake of her life, marrying you. You thought you were doing all right for yourself, didn't you – me and Owen working at the mine, Ma doing her sewing. You thought you could just take it easy. Well, I've had enough. I'm not standing any more of it."

"So what are you going to do about it?" he sneered. "Throw me out with your own hands, is it? Stop ranting, Meg, and take that jug up the tavern and get it filled with beer. My back's too bad to walk up there today."

"Take it yourself," she retorted, "or go without. *I'm* not your slave!"

"Aren't you, by Gow!" Morgan came out of his chair and before Megan could move he had her by the shoulders. His hands were huge and strong. He shook her like a doll and then released one hand to smack her across the face.

"Perhaps that'll teach you to answer me back," he snarled. "There's plenty more where that came from, and if you cheek me again you'll get it. Now take that jug up the tavern and get my beer."

Megan stared at him. I won't do it, she thought. I won't be his skivvy. I won't stay here to have the life crushed out of me like he's crushed it out of Mam.

She turned and ran out of the room, slamming the door behind her.

Megan ran up the street, her cheek still stinging from the slap Morgan had given her. At the corner she paused and looked back, half afraid that he would be following. But apart from one howl of rage as she rushed out, he had done nothing and the door was still closed.

She leaned against the wall, breathing hard. Her heart was kicking against her ribs and she felt sick. Nobody had ever struck her like that before – not Dadda, not Mam, nobody. But she believed Morgan Jones when he threatened he would do it again.

She wandered on along the narrow street. Like most of the pit villages of the Rhondda, the houses were built in long lines along the valley, so that you never had to go far to reach the open mountainside. The mines made great scars in the flanks of the hills, with the black shadows of slag heaps towering above. The air was gritty with coal dust and a dull grey pall hung over the cramped, huddled cottages.

Just outside the village, in an acre or two of garden with a few trees fighting bravely to keep some green amongst the black and grey of coal and granite, stood the house of Ifor Williams, the owner of the mines all along this stretch of the valley. It was a big, grand house with many chimneys and windows, all looking out on the property, and before Megan's mother had married Owen Price, she had been in service there. Sometimes, back in the good old days when Dadda had been alive, when she wasn't tired or worried, she would tell Megan and the others about life in the big house.

"Dinners like you'd never believe in," she would say. "Whole salmon, look, and a leg of lamb it took

15

two men to carry. And the most beautiful laver bread you ever tasted. Live like kings, they do, up at the Big House."

Megan had hardly ever tasted laver bread, the special Welsh delicacy that was made from seaweed, nor lamb, and she had never had salmon at all. Once, her father had taken the boys fishing and come back with a fine one, but he'd only brought it home to show Mam and then he'd taken it straight up to the Big House, for it belonged to them. The river was theirs and everything in it, he said, and they'd only let him fish there as a favour. He'd come back pleased enough with a shilling or two in payment, though, and bought the little ones a handful of broken biscuits from the village shop. That was a bigger treat for them than salmon.

Mam had worked at the Big House from when she was ten years old until she was nineteen. She still went there sometimes, to see the housekeeper, Mrs Gower, and the other maids, and she'd told Megan that Mrs Ifor Williams had spoken to her occasionally and said how much she missed her.

"Nobody can do her hair like I could," she'd said proudly. "I could go back any time and work as a lady's maid again." But when Dadda had died and Megan suggested this, she had shaken her head. "She's had Beth Evans for twenty years now. She'll never change her."

Megan climbed up the hill, away from the straggling line of cottages. There was a path that led

16

away from the clatter of the mines and amongst the rocks and bracken to an old quarry, where the grass grew over the broken earth and a few sheep grazed. You could sit here and look up the valley, towards the mountains of Brecon, and imagine you were miles away from the noise and the dust and the smell of coal.

Megan sat down on a rock and folded her arms around her knees. The sun was dropping towards the western skyline, and the bracken had turned gold with the bite of autumn. There was a scent of frost in the air.

Dadda had been dead for over six months now, and Megan sometimes wondered if her mother had forgotten all about him. His name was never mentioned in the house. But maybe that was because Morgan Jones never left her any time to think about anything. On the run all day long, she was, from four in the morning when she got up to give Owen his breakfast before he went down the pit, till midnight when she finally finished the mounting piles of sewing and dropped into bed again.

And she was looking paler and thinner than ever before. Worse even than she'd looked when Dadda had died.

I've got to do something, Megan thought. I've got to help her get away from that man. I've got to save her.

She thought about her grandmother again. Bronwen Price had been a strong, proud woman who carried herself like a lady, and her husband, Megan's grand-father, had been one of the most respected foremen in the whole of the Rhondda. But he had coughed his life away with the miner's lung disease and left his wife alone, though not badly provided for.

She'd lived by herself for a while in the cottage that she managed somehow to keep as clean as a palace, despite all the dust and grime of the valley air, and she'd earned some money by putting up some of the merchants who came from Swansea and Cardiff and even further afield to do business with the mine masters. And that was how she'd come to meet Arthur Coleman, a businessman from London who had come to visit Ifor Williams and stayed with her several times.

"He's asked me to marry him," she'd told Dilys one day. "He's leaving the mining trade and setting up his own place in London. A hotel, he calls it, but it's just an inn now. We're going to build it up together, see." She'd glanced at her son, uncertain as to how he would take this news. "It's sorry I am to be leaving you all, but we'll come and see you. And you can stay with us in London."

"London!" Dadda had said. "When are we ever likely to go to London?" But although it hadn't been easy for him to see another man in his father's place, whisking his mother away – to *England*, too! – he'd kissed her and wished them both well, and soon Bronwen had become Mrs Coleman, which seemed a queer sort of name for a Welshwoman to have, though it sounded appropriate enough considering she'd spent her life in a coalmining valley. And one morning she and her new husband had boarded the train and set off to start their new life.

There had been one or two letters after that, and then suddenly nothing. And Dilys had said that Grandma hadn't bothered to answer when she'd written to tell her that her son had died, but perhaps she'd never got the letter. Megan was certain that she wouldn't have just forgotten the family, back here in the Rhondda. And she would have been horrified to see them living like this, in such bitter poverty, with Morgan Jones like a parasite working her mother to death.

Perhaps she'd moved away from the inn. Perhaps she was ill.

I'll have to go and see, Megan thought, *I'll have to find her and tell her.*

But how could she get there? London was hundreds of miles away. There was the road, but the coach was expensive and took too long – why, you had to stay at inns on the way. The new track that had been built to take coal from the Rhondda to Cardiff and went across the Chepstow bridge to join up with the famous Great Western Railway meant that the railway was quicker. You could go all the way to London on that, and a lot quicker than by road. But how could a pit girl like her get the money for the fare?

Megan had no money of her own. Every penny she earned went to help with the housekeeping. Sometimes her mother would give her a farthing or even a halfpenny to buy a ribbon with, or a treat for the little ones, but even that hadn't happened since Morgan Jones had come to live with them.

None of their neighbours or friends would be able to help, she knew that. Everyone in the Rhondda was as poor as everyone else. The men and boys worked in the pit, the women toiled up above – some of them even went underground too – and at the end of it all they had barely enough to feed and clothe their families. Nobody had spare money for trips to London. Most of them had never even been as far as Cardiff.

There was only one person Megan could think of who might help. One person with the means, one person who was fond enough of her mother to want to make life easier for her again. To make life *possible*.

Mrs Ifor Williams.

Chapter 4

"You want to see the mistress?" Mrs Gower stared at Megan. A little scullery-maid had brought her into the kitchen where the housekeeper was sitting in a big rocking-chair by the range. Two other maids were working at the long table, preparing vegetables, and in a small room just off the kitchen a boy of about twelve was polishing boots.

"What does a girl like you want with the mistress?" The housekeeper peered more closely. "Here, it's Megan Price, isn't it? Dilys's girl? Sit down on that stool and tell me how your mam is. You used to come here with her, didn't you?"

"That's right, Mrs Gower. Mam used to bring me when I was little." Megan glanced around. The kitchen was like a huge cavern, big enough to get the whole of the Price house in. The *Jones* house now, she reminded herself, and felt the bitterness rise in her throat.

"And are you looking to work here, like your mam did?" Mrs Gower shook her head. "There, it's sorry I am, *bach*. We don't need any more maids now, see. Just taken on two new kitchen girls and a parlour-maid, and Beth Evans won't leave for years yet."

"It's not a job I'm looking for," Megan said. She looked miserably at the housekeeper and then burst out, "It's Mam. You know she got married again after … after Dadda…"

"I heard that, yes." Mrs Gower looked at her kindly. "Morgan Jones, isn't it? Not that I know him myself, mind, but we hear things up here just the same. Not like your dad, is he?"

"He's *nothing* like Dadda," Megan said. "He's just a scrounger. He's stopped going to work, says he's got a bad back, and he just sits in his chair – in *Dadda's* chair – all day and does nothing, while poor Mam slaves away at tailoring. And he drinks. He spends all the money on drink." She screwed up her face in disgust. "He's horrible, Mrs Gower."

The housekeeper stared at her. Then she lifted one hand and touched Megan's cheek. The sting had faded but left a dull ache behind, and felt swollen and tender.

"Did he do that? Been hitting you, has he?" Mrs Gower shook her head. "Does he hit your mam too?"

"No. At least, I don't think so." But Megan stopped, remembering nights when she had heard her mother sobbing after she'd gone to bed. Had Morgan Jones been hitting her then, or was she just regretting that she'd married him? In any case, it wouldn't be long before he started, Megan was sure of that.

"I've got to get help for her," she said. "I want to go to London and find my grandma. She'd help, I know she would, only we haven't heard from her for months. I don't think she even knows that Dadda's dead."

"Bronwen Price? Didn't she get married again? Someone foreign, wasn't it?"

"English." Megan nodded. "He came from London. He has a business there and Grandma went to help him run it. An inn."

"Well, she ought to know about your dadda," Mrs Gower said. "He was her son, after all. And she was always a good mother, Bronwen Price – never one to see her family go in want. You're right, she's the one to help you. But how are you going to get to London, then?"

Megan looked at the floor. Neither of her parents had ever taken "charity". Dadda in particular had always insisted that whatever they had must be worked for and earned. She could almost feel him behind her, frowning in disapproval at what she was doing.

But it's for *Mam*, she thought, almost as if she were talking to him. I'm doing it to help Mam.

"That's why I've come here," she said in a whisper. "I need the money for the fare, you see. I thought perhaps Mrs Williams – with Mam being her maid once…" She thought of her father saying "Neither a borrower nor a lender be", and understood what he had meant. She knew she could never pay it back.

"You came to ask the mistress for the fare to London? It's that desperate you are?"

Megan nodded. "I can't stay in the house with him any longer. I've got to get help."

Mrs Gower frowned and gazed at the range. The coals were glowing, throwing out a warm comfort, and there was a kettle singing softly on the hob. The maids were talking quietly as they worked at the table, in the lilting tones of the Welsh language. Megan wished she could stay here always, in the haven of this comfortable kitchen, and never move again.

"Tell you what I'll do, girl," the housekeeper said suddenly. "Your mam was always a good friend of mine – helped me out more than once, she did, when we were maids together here, years ago. There was a time when I'd have lost my position if it hadn't been for her. I can't stand by now and see her suffer. *I'll* give you the money for your fare, Megan. I'll give you enough to get to London and find your grandma. Bring her back here, let her see what's going on – she'll soon sort it out."

Megan stared at her. "*You'll* give me the money? But – I might never be able to pay it back. I can't—"

"We'll talk about paying back later," Mrs Gower said. "I've got a bit put by. You've got to think about your old age when you're like me. But there's enough to spare you some now, so no arguing, see?" She got up and went out of the room. Megan sat on the little stool and waited. The maids finished their work and went outside with the vegetable peelings.

Mrs Gower came back. She was holding a small leather purse. She sat down again and then opened it, tipping the coins out into her hand.

"There, that should be enough to take you to

London. You've got your grandma's address, have you?"

"Yes." Megan blinked at the money. It was enough to keep the family for a fortnight. "But are you sure? I mean, suppose I can't—"

"You'll do your best. You're Dilys Price's daughter, and your dadda was a good man." The housekeeper gave her the same kind look. "Grew up together we did, the three of us, and your mam and me came here as girls the same day, to start work. Like sisters, we were. Be a shame if I couldn't lift my hand to help her now, wouldn't it?"

Megan left the house, feeling bemused. She walked slowly down the hill, feeling the weight of the purse in her pocket. Enough money to pay her train fare to London! Enough money to help her find her grandmother and ask her help, to rescue her mother from the dreadful position she was in.

Her heart beat fast. She felt excited and scared all at once, at the idea of travelling so far all by herself. And she could scarcely imagine what London would be like. Why, they said it was bigger than Merthyr Tydfil, even bigger than Swansea or Cardiff!

I'll go tomorrow, she decided. First thing in the morning. I'll go out as if I'm going to work and I'll walk to the station instead and get on the train. And by tomorrow evening I'll be there, with Grandma.

Chapter 5

Megan had never travelled on a train. She climbed into the carriage as cautiously as if she were entering the lair of some wild animal, and indeed the engine was just like a huge beast, puffing and snorting as it stood impatiently at the platform. Once or twice it sighed loudly, as if exasperated at having to stop for passengers at all, and when it set off it did so with a jerk that almost toppled Megan from her seat.

She clung to the door, afraid to let go as the carriages gathered speed. Within a few minutes they were rushing, almost frantically it seemed, through the countryside, already leaving the straggling streets behind and dashing through the steep cuttings. The mountains rose above them, sometimes darkened with heaps of slag from mine workings, sometimes green and gold with bracken. Here and there a stream tumbled down the hillside or fell in a bright and glittering cascade over the rocks.

Gradually, Megan released her hold on the door. She stared out, fascinated by the swiftly changing scenes. The train rattled loudly, the carriage swaying as it hurtled round bends, and great clouds of smoke billowed back from the engine, puffing through the open window and covering everything with smuts. Once they were plunged into sudden darkness, and Megan gave a little cry of surprise, but within minutes they were in bright daylight again and, looking back, she could see that they had just come through a tunnel in the hill.

"Never been on a train before, is it?" remarked a comfortable-looking woman sitting opposite with a basket on her knees. "Always a bit of a surprise, the first time."

Megan smiled shyly. She had been afraid that she might be seen by someone she knew, but nobody the Prices knew ever went anywhere by train. And amongst all the hurry of people on their way to work in the morning, nobody had noticed her slip off to the railway station instead of towards the pit.

It would be evening before she was missed. She hadn't told anyone her plans, not even Owen. She had gone back home last night, expecting to be met with fury and recriminations from Morgan Jones, but he was already asleep, snoring in the chair by the fire. He'd made Emlyn go to the tavern for his beer and had drunk most of it before Dilys came home, so they'd sat quietly together, thankful for the peace and taking care not to wake him. Megan had boiled some potatoes for supper and helped her mother with the sewing, and then they'd gone to bed early, leaving Morgan in his chair. At some time in the night, she'd heard him stumble upstairs and had lain awake for a while, her heart hammering, but he must have fallen asleep again as soon as he fell on to the lumpy mattress beside her mother.

In the morning, there'd been little time to talk. Owen was in a hurry to go to work and Dilys was packing up the week's quota of trousers, to take them back to Merthyr Tydfil. She'd be away until the afternoon. The little ones were going next door, where old Nan would look after them along with several other small children whose mothers were at work all day. They sprawled together on a mattress or scuffled outside in the coal dust and mud, waiting for the crust of bread she would give them at midday. Some of the bigger ones, like Emlyn and Dafydd, roamed further afield and only came back when it started to get dark, and Nan didn't bother about them at all.

Megan had left the house just as if she were going to the pit. She'd hesitated on the doorstep for a moment, wanting to say something to her mother before leaving, but she knew that if she did it would make things even worse when Morgan Jones found out. Best if Mam knew nothing. So she hadn't been able to bring anything with her, not even a warmer shawl. All she had was the small leather purse that Mrs Gower had given her, which she'd clutched tightly in her hand all through the night.

The comfortable woman was probably a farmer's wife. She looked as if she was quite used to travelling by train.

"Going far, are you, *bach*?" she enquired. "I'm bound for Chepstow myself, to see my daughter. She's just had a new baby so I'm going to stay for a while and help with the little ones. Five, she's got now, look you, and all boys, would you believe it."

"I'm going to London," Megan said, and the woman opened her eyes wide.

"London! Well, that's an adventure. I've never been across the river myself. Wales is good enough for me."

It's good enough for me too, Megan thought, looking out of the window again. Or was, until Morgan Jones came into the family. She wondered when she would see the mountains again, when she would breathe the gritty air of the valleys with their grey terraced houses lining the slopes and the slag-heaps rising above. There wasn't much beauty there but it was *home*, and she felt a sudden longing to be back, sitting at her father's feet on the rag rug while Owen sang as he washed himself out in the scullery.

But Dadda wasn't there any more. Morgan Jones sat in his chair now, glowering and drinking. And Mam was growing paler and thinner each day, her eyes and fingers sore from the sewing, her face lined with worry and unhappiness.

The Welsh mountains were falling behind now, giving way to the flat wooded plain of the Severn estuary. Ahead lay England, almost a foreign land, and the great, bustling city of London.

Once again, Megan felt a twinge of fear. What was she doing, coming so far, all by herself?

And suppose she couldn't find Grandma after all? Suppose she'd moved away – or even died?

Chapter 6

London was even bigger than Megan had expected. Even in her wildest imaginings she had never pictured this enormous, bustling place with its huge buildings and clattering streets.

And it seemed to go on for ever. The train had passed street after street as it rattled into the city, row after row of houses as small and cramped as the little terraces in the villages of the Rhondda, and then a seemingly never-ending stream of big houses, houses as big as Ifor Williams's or even bigger, and churches that looked like cathedrals with domes and great towers soaring into the dusky sky.

It was almost night when they arrived. The journey had seemed endless. Even London couldn't be as far away as this, she had thought, but at last here they were and the darkness was closing in as the train drew into the station and the passengers got out.

Megan stared about her. The platforms stretched away on either side like wide roads, wider than any in the Rhondda, and above them soared an enormous roof, built of a tracery of wrought-iron and glass and supported by tall, graceful pillars. It was more like a great cathedral or a huge palace than a railway station. It seemed almost a sacrilege to use such a building for trains.

She came out on to the street and looked uncertainly from side to side.

There were people everywhere, hurrying along the pavements as though their lives depended on it – more people than Megan had ever seen in one place. Why, if you brought all the folk of the Rhondda and put them into this one street, it wouldn't be as crowded as it was now! And they didn't speak to each other like the villagers back home in the valleys did. No "*yacchi da*", no cheerful hello. They just bustled past as if they didn't even see each other.

The street was noisy too, so noisy that Megan put her hands to her ears. The clatter of horses' hooves and the rattle of iron wheels echoed and rebounded from the high, solid walls of the buildings. There were tradesmen with carts and wagons, urging their horses on with loud, coarse voices, and coster women calling their wares – flowers, pies, fresh fish, ribbons. There were small boys, as ragged as any Megan had seen in the valleys, dodging in and out between the carts, whistling and shrieking, and there were big, rough-looking youths who stared at her and guffawed.

The din swelled about her and rose in the air, but the buildings were too high to let it escape and it seemed to grow and swirl like the trodden brown leaves that had fallen from the trees lining the pavements. Megan felt as if it were battering at her head, and she looked about her for relief, but she knew that beyond this street was another, and then another and another. This was London and there was no way out. And in any case, she couldn't leave before she had found her grandmother.

She moved away from the youths. The darkening streets were lit by glimmering gas-lamps and a row of hansom cabs stood alongside the pavement, with their drivers sitting high up above the little passenger-cabins. They glanced at Megan and then looked away, obviously realizing that she had no money for a cab. A few old men sat huddled against the wall, their caps on the ground in front of them, evidently begging.

"Lookin' fer someone, ducks?" a voice asked from the darkness beside her, and Megan jumped nervously. She turned and found a short, rather stocky man beside her. He was wearing an old jacket and a waist-coat that had once been richly decorated, and he was smoking a pipe. His voice was as rough as a bucketful of gravel and he spoke in a way Megan had never heard before. She had to ask him to repeat his question twice before she understood.

"No – I mean, yes." She hesitated. Mrs Gower had told her to be careful in London and not to confide in strangers. But what else could you do when you'd never been there before and didn't know anyone? "I'm going to see my grandma," she said. "She lives in Kensington. She's got an inn there."

"An inn! In Kensington!" For some reason, he seemed to find this funny. "Not the Potteries, I 'ope."

He stared at her, his eyes narrowed. "You're not from round 'ere, are yer? Where d'yer come from?"

"Wales. From the Rhondda," she said proudly, but he shook his head.

"Never 'eard of it. Well, I've 'eard of *Wales*, o' course. But not that other place – sounds like a woman's name, that does. So you wants to get ter Kensington, does yer?"

"Yes," she said, wondering if she'd told him too much. He didn't look very clean, but she was used to men looking dirty. *Everyone* looked dirty in the Rhondda – you couldn't help it. It didn't mean you couldn't be trusted.

"Well, you wants ter get on a bus," he said. "There's horse omnibuses, see, what goes all over London. One o' them'll take you to Kensington. Just look fer the sign on the front. It'll cost you a copper or two fer yer fare, that's all."

He turned away and vanished into the darkness. Megan stood helplessly for a moment or two, wondering where to catch an omnibus. Then she saw one coming towards her – a big vehicle drawn by four horses, with a crowd of people aboard it. It even had passengers sitting up on the roof as well, and on the front, just as the man had said, there was a sign.

It didn't say Kensington, though, it said Hammersmith. Megan stood looking at it, chewing her lip and wondering whether it would take her where she wanted to go. Where was Hammersmith? Was it a part of London, or was it somewhere out in the country?

"Well, come on, miss, make up yer mind." The omnibus had stopped and a man was leaning out of it and waving at her. "You comin' with us or not? We ain't got all day."

"I want to go to Kensington."

"Kensington? Nah – don't go nowhere near there. Nor don't none of the buses what goes from 'ere. You wants to cross the road, see, an' wait over on that corner. One'll come along in a bit."

He flipped his reins and the horses moved on. Megan stood uncertainly on the edge of the pavement. To reach the other side of the road, she would have to find a path through a constant procession of vehicles, from dainty governess carts to huge brewery drays, all drawn by horses which varied in size from sharp-hooved ponies to enormous Clydesdales and shires with feet the size of coal-shovels.

It looked as inaccessible as a foreign shore. And for a moment, Megan felt like sitting down on the pavement and crying. But that wouldn't help anyone. And it was no use coming to London if she was going to give up at the first hurdle. So she took her courage firmly in both hands – clenching her fists, just as if she really were holding it tight – and stepped out into the road.

"Oi! Whatcher think yer doin'?" There was a startled neigh and a scraping of hooves, and a flurry of mud sprayed up and spattered itself all over her. "You silly little fool! Look where yer goin', can't yer?" A man was scowling down at her from his seat on the cart that had nearly run her over, and Megan jumped back to the pavement, trembling all over.

"I'm sorry," she began. "I didn't see—" But already the cart was moving away, with the man still cursing, and she pulled herself together and set off again, looking carefully in every direction before daring to take a step.

She reached the far pavement safely at last and stood for a moment getting back her breath before turning towards the corner where she would catch the omnibus. She still had a little money in the purse Mrs Gower had given her – enough, she hoped, for the fare to Kensington. And she had the name of her grandmother's inn written down on a scrap of paper in the same little purse. She felt in her pocket for it now, reassured by the soft leather in her fingers. Surely it couldn't be long before she was there, telling Grandma all about Dadda's terrible accident and Morgan Jones, and then everything would be all right.

But although she stood at the corner for a long time, the omnibus to Kensington never arrived. And when she asked a woman passing by when it would come, all she got was a pitying stare and a laugh.

"There won't be no more buses to Kensington tonight, ducks! Gorn 'ome to their beds, that's where they'll all be. You'll 'ave ter wait till mornin' now."

Morning! Megan gazed at her in dismay.

What was she to do all night? Where could she go?

Chapter 7

Never in all her life had a night seemed so long, nor so cold. After the woman had told her there would be no more buses until morning, Megan turned away from the corner where the wind scurried about like a thief, trying to whip away her skirts and shawl, lifting the bonnet from her head.

She walked aimlessly down the street, wondering what to do next. There might be enough money in her purse for a night's lodging somewhere, but until she knew what it would cost to get to Kensington she was afraid to spend anything. And she was nervous of finding lodgings. Megan had never slept anywhere but in her own home, and the thought of staying amongst strangers was as bad as that of roaming the streets.

In the streets! Was that really what she would have to do – spend the night wandering these dark, noisy chasms between the huge buildings that reared so threateningly on every side?

It was like being in the mountains, she thought, glancing up at the great stone walls; like being in one of the steep hidden canyons or secret valleys. But she would have felt safer there, knowing that there was nothing to harm her, only the buzzards and the fork-tailed red kites and the wild Welsh ponies.

Here, she seemed to be surrounded by menace, by cavernous alleyways that led into unknown depths, by scurrying figures that looked only half-human in the shifting darkness, by sounds that were strange to her ears. And every face that loomed out of the darkness glimmered a sickly greenish-white in the gaslight, like a ghost or the gargoyles that she had seen on the gutterings of Ifor Williams's house.

A door opened suddenly and light flooded out on to the pavement. Megan stopped and listened. There was a boisterous roar of laughter from within, and then a girl stumbled out on to the pavement, clutching a flower-decked hat to her dark head. She looked over her shoulder and called out something, and then the door closed behind her and she turned and bumped straight into Megan.

"Oi! What you doin', standin' 'ere in the dark? You nearly 'ad me in the gutter." She stopped and peered into Megan's face. "I 'ope yer not thinkin' of stealin' my pitch? I does all along this street, see? We don't want no one else down 'ere."

"I'm not doing anything," Megan said. The girl looked a year or two older than her, plump and pretty in a blowsy sort of way, with black curls that swung round her face, and red lips. She was wearing a red dress with a low, frilly neckline, and a shawl draped carelessly over her shoulders. "I've only just come to London. I'm trying to find my way to Kensington."

37

"Kensington! Well, this ain't the way. You wants to go back and catch a bus, that's what you wants to do. Only there won't be no more buses now, not till morning."

"I know." Megan gazed helplessly at the girl. "I don't know what to do. I suppose I'll have to find somewhere to stay, but I haven't got much money. And I don't know where to go."

"Cor, you ain't 'alf in a state!" the girl said. She looked at Megan consideringly. "Where d'you come from, then?"

"Wales." She didn't mention the Rhondda this time. "I've come to find my grandmother."

"An' she lives in Kensington, does she? Well, you can't get there till morning, that's certain." The girl thought for a moment. "Wales, you say? Do they all talk like you there?"

"I suppose so." Megan had never thought about the way she talked, but she'd noticed at once that Londoners had a very different way of speaking. It sounded harsh to her after the soft, lilting voices she was used to. And the singing she'd heard was raucous, though the tune had been plain enough.

"I 'eard a bloke talk like you once," the girl said. "And 'e could sing too, sing like a bird. Can you sing?"

Megan shook her head helplessly. Everyone could sing, surely? It came as naturally as speaking. The miners sang on their way to the pits, the girls sang as they unloaded the skips. It was a way of getting through the tedium of the work.

"I bet you can," the girl said, staring at her. "Go on. Sing us something now."

Megan racked her brains. She felt as if she had strayed into a dream, that she couldn't really be standing here on a dark London pavement being urged to sing by a girl she had never seen before. She would wake up soon, wake up and find that none of it had ever happened – that her mother had never married Morgan Jones, that Dadda was still alive and getting ready to go to the pit…

But the tears that suddenly clogged her throat told her that it was no dream, that it had all happened and that her mother would even now be wondering where she had gone, finding the note she had left and giving it to Owen to read to her, that Morgan Jones would be erupting into fury.

Sing? How could she sing? But there was nothing else she could do, for the time being. She couldn't reach her grandmother until morning, and meanwhile this girl did seem to be friendly. And what would happen to her if she turned away?

The songs of her homeland came into her mind: *Myfanwy* and *The Bells of Aberdovey*. The tears stung her eyes as she lifted her voice, and sounded through the words. And even though she sang in Welsh and her listeners could not understand, the purity of her singing brought the men and women to the door of the tavern to listen to her. And when she had finished, there was a moment's silence before they broke into cheers.

"You *can* sing an' all," the dark girl said. "I knew you would. 'Ere, I'll tell you what we'll do. You can come along of me, do a few turns in the drinkin'-'ouses, see, an' see 'ow much we can pick up. Then you can come back to my place an' doss down for the rest of the night. 'T ain't much, but it's better'n puttin' up in a doorway."

"Sing, you mean? For money?"

"Thassit. Sing for yer supper." The girl laughed. "What's yer name? Mine's Sally."

"Megan. Megan Price." Mam had tried to get her to call herself Megan Jones but she'd refused.

"Megan. That's a queer name. I'll call yer Meg," Sally decided, and led the way through the tavern door. "They're a mean lot in 'ere," she confided, her black eyes laughing. "Couldn't get no more'n tuppence-ha'penny out of the lot of 'em. Let's see what you can do."

Megan never knew afterwards how many drinking-houses they visited, she and Sally. She could only remember a blur of crowded rooms smelling of beer, a throng of Cockney faces, a steady bellow of conversation, of laughter and quarrelling and, above all, the singing. Sally singing her lively, raucous music-hall songs, and Megan herself bringing a hush to the bustling taverns with her Welsh ballads.

Land of My Fathers, *David of the White Rock*, and the beautiful songs which meant so much to the Welsh – *Myfanwy* and *Bread of Heaven* – all these and more came softly from her throat, and even the roughest Cockney paused in his drinking to listen to words he did not understand with an unexpected moisture in his eyes.

"Well, that was a turn-up an' no mistake," Sally said afterwards, leading Megan through the darkened streets. The gas-lamps had been turned off now and there was only the faintest of glows from the sky to show them the way. The narrow side streets were cluttered with piles of rubbish and Megan stumbled several times, but Sally was as sure-footed as a goat.

"This is where I live." She stopped and pushed open a creaking door which led into a dark passage-way. It smelt of old cabbage and dirt, but Sally didn't seem to notice it. She led the way along the passage and down a short flight of stairs, slippery with grime.

"Got me own place, I 'ave," she said proudly and moved away to attend to something. A moment later, a candle flared and Megan blinked and looked around her.

They were in a cellar. It was hardly bigger than a cupboard, with blackened walls streaked with damp and green fungus growing in one corner. On the floor was an old mattress covered with sacking and tattered blankets, and beside it there was a cracked plate with a lump of bread on it, and a cup with several chips out of its rim.

"All right, ain't it?" Sally said, and Megan nodded. Somehow, she had expected Londoners to be richer and better housed than the people she had grown up with in the Rhondda valleys, but already she was

41

beginning to realize that there was just as much poverty here as she had left behind.

They said the streets of London were paved with gold, she thought, but it's no more than the gold you're supposed to find at the end of the rainbow. There's no gold anywhere for the likes of us.

Sally took a small bottle from her pocket and poured a trickle of watered ale into the cup. She drank some and handed the rest to Megan. Then she cut the bread into two hunks. The two girls sat down on the mattress.

"We done well tonight," Sally declared. "Do ourselves proud termorrer. A slap-up breakfast we'll 'ave, 'am an' eggs, sausages – the lot. There's a bake'ouse round the corner, opens at six." She held her stomach. "I can't wait!"

Megan was hungry too. She had had nothing all day but a scrap of cold potato she had brought from home. With Morgan Jones's eye on her, she hadn't dared take anything more out of the house than she would have taken to the pit, so she had come with only her usual dinner and her shawl to wrap around her. She chewed the stale bread as if it were manna from heaven, and the thought of a breakfast such as Sally had described made her mouth water.

"So what d'yer think?" Sally asked, and Megan realized she had been talking. "Shall we team up? I bin lookin' fer a partner ever since our Susie popped it." She looked at Megan. "You could live 'ere with me. Better'n goin' to yer gran in Kensington."

42

Megan stared at her. "Live here? Go singing with you every night? Is that what you mean?"

"Well, I ain't askin' yer to marry me!" Sally retorted, and laughed. "You won't get a better offer, mind. Reg'lar work an' a place to live. It ain't summat to sneeze at."

"But I can't. I've got to find Grandma. You see..." Megan hesitated. Mrs Gower had told her not to tell her story to strangers. But Sally wasn't a stranger, was she? She had already proved herself to be a friend. She'd even helped her earn some money. "I've got to find her," she said again, too tired to talk any more.

"Well, thass all right," Sally said. "We'll go to Kensington an' find 'er. An' then you can come back 'ere an' live with me."

Megan knew that she couldn't. She had to find Grandma and then go back to the valley to help her mother escape from Morgan Jones. But once again she had that strange feeling that she was wandering in a dream, and as she ate her dry bread and drank the ale Sally had given her, she felt her eyes close and reality slip away from her.

She slid down on the mattress, fast asleep.

Chapter 8

"I can't," Megan said for the umpteenth time. "I can't stay here with you. I've told you, I've got to find Grandma."

Sally stared at her. In the cold, pale light of morning she looked older than she had last night, her face washed out and her eyes smudged with tiredness. The bounce had gone from her step, and her voice was dejected as she said, "But I need you, Meg. You saw what it was like last night. They're tired of the old songs, the ones I know. They wants something new — something a bit out of the ordinary. An' they liked you. You 'ad 'em in the palm of yer 'and."

"I could teach you some more of my songs," Megan said. She had taught Sally one or two of her favourite Welsh ballads last night, and they had sung them together. But the other girl shook her head.

"It won't be the same. I ain't got the right voice. You need that sort of lilt like you've got. You need to be Welsh."

Megan sighed. She didn't want to let her new friend down, but she had to do what she had come to London for. She couldn't think of Mam still slaving away for that idler Morgan Jones and for all the little ones, and not do her best to help them.

"You could earn some money," Sally said wheedlingly. "You could send it 'ome. Wouldn't that do?" Megan had told her about the family and Morgan Jones as they ate the breakfast Sally had promised her. "You'd earn more singin' in London than back in the mines."

For a moment or two, Megan was tempted. She had been astonished at the amount they had collected last night – as much as she earned in a week from her job at the pit. But she'd also been dismayed at the cost of the breakfast. Everything was more expensive in London, Sally told her. You needed to earn more, just to stay the same.

"It's not just money," she said. "I've got to get Mam away from him. He's a brute, Sally, but she won't leave him unless she's got somewhere else to go, and she can't throw him out now he's her husband."

The other girl sighed. "Well, tell me where yer gran lives anyway. I might want to go up Kensington way meself sometime. Runs an inn, does she? We might get some business there. What's its name?"

"I can never remember. Something about bells – the Ring o' Bells, or the Bellringer, is it?" Megan fished the little leather purse out of her pocket. Amongst the few coins she still had left from the train fare was the scrap of paper with her grandmother's name and address on. "She's Mrs Coleman now – she used to be Price, of course, but after Grandad died she got married again, see, to Mr Coleman and he brought her back to

London to help run the inn, and—" Megan stopped, wondering why she had begun to chatter so much. Perhaps it was because she felt suddenly nervous at the thought of setting out through London again, all alone. She wished Sally could come with her. "Here's its name. The Twelve Bells."

Sally took the scrap of paper and nodded. "I'll show you where to catch the bus. Mind you come back and see us. We could do well, you an' me, singin' round the pubs. Better'n workin' in a dirty old mine."

Megan half agreed with her. It had been fun singing the songs she loved so much, seeing the people fall silent as her voice rose above their chatter. It had been exciting to hear their roars of appreciation, and to see them toss pennies into the bag that Sally held out. But she didn't think she wanted to do that for the rest of her life. They might be poor in the valleys, but the air in the mountains was clean, and away from the pits it was quiet and peaceful with just the mew of the buzzard to be heard in the clear blue sky. In London there was no escape from the noise and bustle, from the dirt of the streets and the grittiness of the air.

The two girls left the bakehouse and walked along the street. Although it was early, there were plenty of people about: tradesmen delivering goods to the backs of shops and warehouses, boys dashing along the pavements on errands, women scrubbing steps or trudging off with shopping baskets over their arms. The smell of rotting vegetables hung in the air, and Megan turned her head aside as she passed a dead dog lying in the gutter.

46

On the main road, a street-sweeper was moving slowly along with his cart, scraping up the rubbish that had been left about, and some of the shopkeepers were washing down the pavement outside their windows with stiff brooms. The air was bitterly cold, with a biting wind which sliced through the narrow streets, and the girls drew their shawls more closely around them.

"There it is," Sally said suddenly, and Megan saw the omnibus coming along the road towards them. This time the notice on the front did say Kensington, and she waved at it with relief. The horses clattered to a stop and she looked at Sally, feeling suddenly desolate.

"It's all right," Sally said, giving her a push. "You know where I am an' I know where you're goin'. We can find each other again. You go off an' find yer gran, and when you've got yer ma and the kids all sorted out you can come back, see, an' we'll set up together. Might even go on the 'alls! 'Ow about that, eh?" She laughed, but Megan could see that she was struggling to keep back her own tears. Perhaps she was as lonely and friendless as Megan herself. Perhaps even when you'd lived in London all your life, you could still be frighteningly alone.

Megan scrambled aboard and found a seat. She sat looking out, watching the streets nervously as the omnibus rattled along. The conductor came along and asked where she wanted to go, and she stared at him dumbly.

"Come on, miss, we ain't got all day. Where d'yer

47

want to get off?"

"Kensington. Don't you go to Kensington?"

"Says so on the front, dunnit? But that ain't the only stop, and it's a different fare for every one. Now, where's it ter be? Kensington Road, Kensington 'igh, Kensington Square, the Work'ouse or what? It's fer you ter say."

Megan's head reeled. She had no idea where her grandmother's inn was, only that it was Kensington. She looked into her purse and drew out a penny.

"How far will that take me?"

He shrugged. "Take yer to the 'igh, that will. The 'igh Street," he added, seeing that she didn't understand him. "That's probably the best place fer you ter get off anyway." He dropped the penny into his own leather bag and gave her a scrap of paper. "There's yer ticket."

"How will I know when we're there?" she asked desperately, but he had already turned away and was talking to another passenger.

However, she soon discovered that the conductor called out the name of every stop and made sure that no one travelled further than they had paid for. Relaxing a little, she turned again to look out of the window, and exclaimed with astonishment.

"Why, surely to goodness that's a mine! I didn't know there were mines in London."

At the sound of her own voice, she blushed, feeling that everyone on the bus must have turned to stare at her. She glanced round and found a plump woman sitting next to her, smiling. Megan blushed deeper.

"I'm sorry, I forgot I was on my own. But I was so surprised, like, seeing a mine in the middle of London…"

"Bless you, ducks, that ain't a mine," the woman said, chuckling. "That's the new underground railway they're diggin'. See, they're goin' to 'ave trains goin' all over the city – well, all *under* it, I suppose I should say." She shook her head. "They've just started it. Costin' a fortune, it is. Knocked down goodness knows 'ow many 'ouses to dig it, too. They say they'll build more – but I'll believe that when it 'appens. And you'll never get *me* on it. Goin' underground! It'll be 'orrible."

"It *is* horrible," Megan said, thinking of the mines. "I shouldn't think anyone would want to use it."

"Well, that's what I say. They'll never get no one down there. White elephant, that's what that'll turn out to be." The omnibus was slowing down and she got up, swaying a little. "Well, this is my stop, Kensington 'igh Street. Cheerio, ducks."

Kensington High Street! Megan jumped up and followed her. She stepped down from the omnibus and stood on the pavement, gazing about her at yet another crowded street, yet another canyon of enormous buildings. How many people were there in London? she wondered. How did a place get so big?

The plump woman had vanished into the crowd. Uncertain which direction to take first, Megan gazed up and down the street. There was an inn close beside her, but it wasn't called the Ring o' Bells. It had a picture of a queen on its sign. The Queen's Head – there was a tavern called that in the next village to Megan's. And not much further along the busy street, there was another – The Talbot. It had a dog on its sign, with a bird in its jaws. There was nowhere which was anything to do with bells.

Megan wandered on. Perhaps it was in one of the side streets. She glanced down them as she passed. Some were quite wide and almost as busy as the main road, others narrow and dank, as if they never got any sun. Their walls were black with the grime of the smoky air, their gutters running with thick slime. A few ragged children rolled about in the mud, and men and women lounged against the walls, turning to stare as Megan paused.

"Seen enough, 'ave yer?" one woman called to her, and Megan flushed and hurried on. Surely her grand-mother's inn couldn't be in one of these dreadful places?

Suddenly her heart leapt. Ahead of her was yet another tavern, no better than any of the others with its scarred walls and peeling paintwork, but above its door, swinging and creaking in the bitter wind, was a sign with a bell on it.

The Bellmaker.

Megan gazed at it excitedly. She went to push open the door, then hesitated. Was that the name? She'd never been able to remember properly. She fumbled in her pocket and pulled out the little leather purse.

"*Oi! Watch it, mate!*"

Megan gave a cry of alarm as a man suddenly

50

cannoned into her, his heavy body almost knocking her off her feet. She was grabbed by two big hands and saved from toppling into the gutter, then held as she stumbled and regained her balance. Startled and frightened, she looked up into a big, whiskery face with bloodshot eyes, and screamed again.

"'Ere, 'ere, no need to set up a caterwaul like that," the man said roughly. "I was on'y tryin' ter stop yer gettin' run down. If you'd stood there a minute longer you'd've bin under that dray what just went past. Did'ncher see it?"

Megan shook her head. She had had no idea she was in the way of the traffic – she'd thought herself safe on the pavement. She looked at the heavy dray now clattering away along the road and shuddered, thinking of herself under the huge dinner-plate hooves of the big horse.

"I'm sorry – I didn't realize –" she stammered, and he shrugged and let her go.

"Thass all right, gal. No 'arm done. But you be a bit more careful, see? There won't always be someone like me, ready to 'elp a damsel in distress."

He walked away and Megan gazed after him. Her heart was still hammering with fright. She turned and looked at the inn sign again.

Where was the scrap of paper with her grandmother's address on it? She felt again in her pocket for the little purse and then dismay trickled like ice over the whole of her body.

The leather purse had gone.

Chapter 9

It took Megan only a few moments to realize what had happened. She had never really been in danger from the brewer's dray. The man had come out of the tavern, seen her take her purse from her pocket and deliberately bumped into her, snatching it away as he pretended to save her. She had been robbed, not only of her grandmother's address, but also of the last few pennies she possessed.

She looked up at the inn sign again. The Bellmaker. It didn't really matter after all about the robbery. She had only to go through that door and she would see her grandmother, her own Grandma, who would take her in and help her and tell her what to do about Morgan Jones...

Megan pushed open the door.

Even though it was still only mid-morning, the place was almost full, with men and women crowded around a few benches and a couple of girls dashing backwards and forwards with tankards and jugs. Everyone seemed to be talking at once, shouting, arguing, cackling with laughter. The air was thick with tobacco smoke and the smell of beer.

"Well, are you comin' in or not?" a man demanded from the nearest bench. "Make up yer mind. There's a bloomin' gale comin' through that door."

Megan shut the door hastily. Her eyes sought the crowded room for the familiar face of her grandmother, but the only person behind the bar seemed to be a scrawny, gaunt-faced woman with a mouth that was drawn in tightly over toothless gums and a nose and chin so hooked they seemed almost to meet. Her glance passed across Megan indifferently, then returned with more interest. She called one of the serving girls over and muttered something in her ear.

Megan's heart leapt. There must be something about her that the woman had recognized. Could her grandmother have described her, shown her a picture perhaps? The Prices had been too poor to afford photographs, but one of the men in the village had a talent for drawing, and had done sketches for a halfpenny a time. Megan's father had had the whole family drawn as a group once, and given it to his mother when she remarried, as a wedding present. Perhaps she had hung it on the wall somewhere, or displayed it to the women who worked for her.

The serving girl was pushing her way across the crowded room towards her. She had thin, mousy hair and a face as sharp as a ferret's. She looked Megan up and down and spoke shortly, as if she didn't like being sent with messages.

"The old woman wants ter know what you want."

Her voice was sharp too, as if someone had hacked

pieces off it with a blunt saw. She waited impatiently for Megan to answer.

"I'm looking for my grandmother. Her name's Mrs Coleman. She runs an inn called the Bell—"

"Never 'eard of 'er."

The girl spoke curtly. She looked Megan up and down, a sneer curling her lips. "There ain't no one round 'ere called Coleman. You'd better go back where you come from."

Megan felt a rising panic. "But she does live here, I know she does! Can't you ask someone? I've got to find her."

"I told you, there's no one 'ereabouts of that name, leastways not runnin' a pub. The old woman 'ere's called Mrs Crowther, always 'as bin. It ain't no use you arskin' neither; she'll on'y tell you same as what I've done."

She moved forwards, as if to push Megan towards the door. But Megan shook her off, feeling suddenly angry. This girl wasn't any older than she was, and had no right to shove her about. She pushed back, and the girl staggered against a bench and knocked against one of the tankards.

"Oi! Watch what yer doin'," snarled the man whose beer she had spilt. "You better fill it up again or I'll 'ave the law on yer for givin' short measure."

The girl gave Megan a murderous look and snatched up the tankard. She pushed her way back to the bar and slammed the tankard on the counter. Megan followed in time to hear her words to the hook-nosed old woman.

"She's not from round 'ere. Talks funny like she's singin', an' says she's lookin' for 'er gran. Thought she might be runnin' this place."

The woman's eyes moved past her and rested on Megan's face. They were small, hard eyes the colour of Welsh slate and they were narrowed speculatively. She refilled the tankard and pushed it back.

"Take that to the gennelman, an' be more careful next time." She ignored the girl's sulky scowl and spoke to Megan. "Come 'ere, ducks. Lookin' for yer gran, is that right?"

"Yes." Megan moved closer. "She's Welsh, like me, but her name's Mrs Coleman and she runs an inn somewhere in Kensington. It's called the – the –" she racked her brains – "well, there's a bell in the name, and I thought it must be this one, but if it isn't perhaps you could tell me if there are any others around here. I've got to find her, see. Come all the way from the Rhondda I have, on the train."

"On the train, eh?" The old woman looked thoughtful. "An' what'll you do if you can't find 'er?"

"I don't know." Megan had never even considered the possibility that she might not find her grand-mother. "I don't know what I'll do," she repeated, feeling suddenly frightened.

The fear showed in her voice. The old woman put her head on one side. "Got the money for the fare 'ome?"

"No," Megan whispered miserably. "I haven't got any money at all. Someone stole my purse, see – right outside, on the pavement. A man – he bumped into me, nearly knocked me over, and when he'd gone I realized he'd taken it out of my hand." Tears filled her eyes. She knew now that her grandmother wasn't here, that she'd have to start all over again. Suppose she never found her!

The woman clicked her tongue. "Pinched your money, did 'e? That's terrible, that is. You can't trust no one these days. I dunno what the world's comin' to." She looked at Megan again and seemed to make up her mind. "Tell yer what. I'm Aggie Crowther, see, an' I run this place on me own, my dear hubby 'avin' passed on ten years ago. I'm a bit short-handed today, see – one of me gals never turned up this mornin'. 'Ow'd yer like to stop on a bit and give us an 'and? I'll pay yer and give yer a bit o' dinner, and then we'll see what we can do about findin' yer gran."

"Oh, yes." Megan seized the chance gratefully. The thought of going out into the street again, penniless and alone, was too frightening, and to be able to earn some money as well as some food, and then have the woman's help in finding her grandmother, was like a gift. "What do you want me to do?"

"Well, it's the crocks mostly – wants washin', see." Aggie Crowther lifted a flap in the bar and beckoned Megan through to the other side. Feeling very self-conscious, Megan followed her into a dark, cluttered kitchen at the back of the inn. There were two or three other people there – a cook stirring a huge pot on an old range, a skinny girl of about twelve who

56

was standing at a wide, shallow sink scouring hopelessly at a pile of dishes, and a loose-mouthed boy rolling a barrel in from the yard.

"This is where we needs 'elp," Mrs Crowther said. "Poor little Etty, she can't 'ardly manage on 'er own, an' Betsy's got enough to do makin' the stew. We serves food as well, y'see – good nourishin' stew with plenty o' meat in. You won't get a better dinner this side o' the river, you arsk anyone. Old Betsy's knowed all over London for 'er stews."

Megan took off her shawl. The kitchen was steamy but a bitter wind came in through the open door and prevented it from getting warm. She looked at the girl who was still toiling at the sink.

"Shall I do the washing?" she offered. "It'll give you a rest."

The cook looked round and snorted.

"Rest? The likes of us don't get no rest. Get on with the washin' by all means, and young Etty can 'elp me with the veg. There's spuds 'ere needs peelin', an' carrots ter scrub, and that's just to start with. We'll 'ave three or four dozen 'ungry blokes in 'ere soon, all wantin' their dinner, and the devil take us all if it ain't ready for 'em!"

Three or four dozen! There must be almost that many in the taproom now, Megan thought as she plunged her hands into the greasy water. It was barely warm but she knew already that it was useless to ask for hot. No wonder poor Etty had been scrubbing so hopelessly.

But it was her only chance of earning some money and, more importantly, of finding her grandmother. It was quite possible that Aggie Crowther might know her, or even if she didn't would be able to find someone who did. Perhaps by this very evening she would be safe with Grandma and her new husband, telling them all about Morgan Jones.

For the rest of the day she stood at the sink, washing pans and bowls and dishes as fast as the other girls could bring them through to her. The cook's estimation of forty or fifty hungry men seemed to be only a fraction, considering the amount of stew that was cooked and served, and there was no lull in the demand. Three times Betsy sent Ben, the slack-mouthed boy, out for more scrag-end, and the pile of potatoes and carrots for Etty to scrub seemed to get bigger rather than smaller. But at last, long after darkness had fallen and when Megan thought her back must be about to break, Aggie Crowther came through from the taproom and announced that they were closing for the night.

"I've 'ad enough," she said, picking up a leftover hunk of bread and chewing on it. "Up at five we'll be, and startin' again for the breakfast trade. Get some grub down yer an' then get off to yer beds."

Betsy had already tipped the remains of the stew into six bowls and had sat down to eat. Clarrie and Ruth, the other serving girl, came in white and exhausted, and slumped into old chairs at the table, shovelling their food into their mouths with their fingers. Etty gave the floor a perfunctory sweep and joined them.

Megan hesitated at the sink, and Aggie gave her a sharp look.

"Well, miss? Lost yer appetite? It's bin good enough for 'alf London today; don't say it's not good enough for you."

"Oh, yes – yes, it's good." Megan sat down quickly and helped herself to a bowl. But hungry as she was, she couldn't enjoy the stew. The smell of it had been in her nostrils all day and she felt sickened by the taste. Nevertheless, she forced it down her throat, knowing she would feel worse if she didn't eat.

But she was more worried about where she was to sleep that night than about her supper. And about her grandmother. She'd thought that by now she would be with her, yet she seemed no nearer to discovering her whereabouts. What was she to do?

She glanced at Aggie Crowther and the hook-nosed woman seemed to read her thoughts. Her thin lips widened in a crooked smile, and she reached out a skinny hand and patted Megan's arm.

"Don't you fret, ducks. I 'aven't forgot. I bin arskin' people all day if they've 'eard of your gran, an' I think there's a chance that one o' me regulars knows 'er. 'E'll be in again tomorrow, see, an' we'll see what 'e can tell us then, all right?"

Megan nodded, relief almost choking her. Of course he must know Grandma! There couldn't be many Welshwomen in Kensington. And tomorrow he would come and tell Megan just where to find her.

Tomorrow. But – what about tonight?

"You can sleep along of Etty," Aggie said, reading her mind again. "It ain't Buckingham Palace, but it's good enough. Oh, an' you can 'elp out tomorrow as well till this bloke comes in – earn yourself a bit o' breakfast."

Nothing was mentioned about money but Megan was too tired to say anything. She followed Etty upstairs to the tiny attic, wanting only to lie down and sleep. She barely noticed its plainness, nor even the icy draught that found its way in through every crack in the roof. Too worn out even to take off her shoes, she lay down on the lumpy straw mattress beside Etty, rolled herself in her shawl, and slept.

Chapter 10

Megan woke next morning to find herself stiff with cold, her fingers and toes aching. Outside she heard a clock strike five. It was still dark and would be for another two hours or more, but already the street was beginning to bustle with the sounds of hurrying footsteps and the clatter of hooves.

She heard a voice shouting from down below and felt Etty stir and groan beside her. There was a fumbling sound and then a candle guttered into life, casting a feeble, flickering glow around the tiny attic.

"Do we have to get up already?" she asked, rubbing her sore eyes. "I don't seem to have been asleep five minutes."

"Soon as the clock strikes old Aggie's out of bed and bawlin' for the rest of us," the other girl replied. She was sitting up in bed shivering, her shawl wrapped tightly around her thin body. "You ain't come to no rest 'ome 'ere, you know."

Megan glanced around the attic. It was icy cold, with bitter draughts seeping in through the cracked roof. Rain and snow would blow through there too. No wonder Etty had a cough. Megan had noticed it several times yesterday and again in the night. It was a bad one, too. She'd heard miners with coughs like that, and knew that all too often they never got better.

"You ought to take some physic for that," she said as Etty coughed again, crouching over to clutch her chest as if it hurt. But the other girl shook her head.

"It wouldn't do no good," she gasped. "It's right down on me chest, see. It'll be better when I'm up and about."

She got out of bed. Both girls had slept in their clothes and there was no water in the attic, so there was nothing to do but go downstairs, where they found Betsy already blowing life into the fire in the range and the boy, Ben, carrying out the ashes.

"Stir yourselves," Aggie commanded, marching into the kitchen. "Get that kettle boilin', Bet, we all wants a drink o' good 'ot tea to get us started. You girls, cut some bread; there's plenty left from yesterday. An' if there's any stew left over I'll 'ave it. I'm fair shrammed this mornin'."

She rubbed her bony claw-like hands together to warm them, and gave Megan a sharp glance. "Daresay you're used to cold where you're from."

"Only in winter," Megan said. "I've never known it as cold as this."

"An' worse to come, I don't doubt," Aggie said. "Feller in 'ere yesterday reckoned this was goin' to be a real freeze-up. Talkin' about the Thames freezin' over, 'e was! Well, there'll be a good few folk won't see the spring, that's certain, but it won't 'elp to stand

62

around moanin' about it. Is that kettle boilin' yet, Betsy?"

The cook poured strong brown tea into the big chipped cups and they all sat down round the table to drink, dipping yesterday's stale bread in the tea to soften it. Aggie finished up the bowl of stew that was all that had been left, sucking it through her toothless gums. She darted sharp looks at Megan as she ate.

"You can try yer 'and at servin' today," she said suddenly. "The customers like to see a different face. You'll 'ave to be quick on yer feet, mind – no dilly-dallyin'. Think yer up to it?"

"Well … yes, I suppose so." Megan glanced uncomfortably at the other two girls, who were watching her jealously. "But I do have to find my grandmother—"

"That'll keep. I told you, there's a bloke comes in 'ere reg'lar, 'e thinks 'e knows 'er. You'll 'ave to wait till 'e comes in again, and I can't afford idle 'ands around the place. Besides, I thought you said you 'adn't got no dosh."

"I haven't, but—"

"There you are, then. Gotta work for yer livin', aincher? Same as the rest of us." Aggie got to her feet. "It's nearly six. I'll be openin' the doors soon. We serves 'am an' eggs an' fried bread for breakfast, Meg, an' they're all in a 'urry, so you'll 'ave to be nippy on yer pins."

The customers began to filter in as soon as Aggie opened the doors, and soon the three serving girls were running backwards and forwards with plates piled with piping hot fried food. Megan, still famished despite her chunk of tea-sodden bread, felt her saliva begin to run at the smell, but there was no chance of slipping anything into her own mouth. Aggie's eyes were as sharp as a hawk's, and if she didn't spot Megan slide a bit of fried bread or a scrap of bacon into her mouth, one of the other girls would.

They were allowed a short break in the middle of the morning and Megan joined the others in finishing up the last few scraps of ham, wiping the plate clean of fat with another slab of bread. Then it was time to start preparing the stew, and she found herself at the table with Clarrie, the ferret-faced serving girl, scraping carrots.

Neither of them spoke for a while, then Clarrie said, "I thought you were supposed to be lookin' for your gran."

"I am," Megan said. "Mrs Crowther knows someone who might know her. I've got to wait till he comes in."

Clarrie stared at her and then gave a crow of laughter. "She told you that? An' you believed 'er? Cor, you must be still wet be'ind the ears! She ain't goin' ter find your gran for you. She just wants a bit o' cheap labour."

"What do you mean? She promised me—"

"Promises are like piecrust," Clarrie said darkly. "Easy broken. I never take no count of promises."

"You mean she won't? But she *said*—"

"People say all sorts o' things," Clarrie said. "It don't

mean they're true. I dunno what it's like where you come from, but you'll 'ear more lies round 'ere than I've 'ad 'ot dinners." She looked at the carrot in her hands and snorted. "Not that I've 'ad many of *them*."

Megan said nothing. She went on with her work, thinking over what Clarrie had said. Could she trust her? Yesterday the girl had been openly unfriendly, glowering at her whenever she came into the kitchen and jogging her arm more than once as if to make Megan drop a dish or tureen. Perhaps her apparent friendliness now was just a trick to make her leave the inn without waiting for the customer to come in with news of her grandmother.

Before she could say any more, the back door was pushed open and a tall boy of about seventeen, with curly light-brown hair staggered in, carrying a large basket in his arms. He dumped it on the table and stood back, grinning and wiping his brow.

"There you are, ladies. There's your daily bread, so give thanks for it. All fresh and hot, straight from the bakehouse."

"Thanks!" Clarrie sniffed. "Precious little *we'll* get of it till it's too stale for the customers – not that it takes long to go stale. You want to get your dad to buy some fresh yeast, Tom Bradley, an' some good flour too – not stuff crawlin' with weevils."

"Go on," the boy said, grinning. "That's fresh meat, those weevils. You won't get fresher. What's more, they're free. We never charge for weevils!"

"I should just think you wouldn't neither," Clarrie

said indignantly, but her indignation didn't ring true, and Megan noticed a blush on her cheeks that hadn't been there before, and a bright sparkle in her eye. "You'd better take yourself off, Tom Bradley, before you an' me has words."

Tom laughed. He noticed Megan and gave her a friendly wink. "Who's this then? A new slave? Where did old Aggie find you? I haven't seen you round these parts before."

"I've only just arrived," Megan told him shyly. "I'm from Wales." She looked at him, liking his bright, open face and blue eyes. His smile was nice too, showing regular, white teeth. Megan had never seen anyone with teeth that looked clean and strong like his did. Most people had lost at least one or two by the time they reached eighteen.

"From Wales?" he said. "Is that why you talk like that – as if you're singing?"

Megan felt her own cheeks warm with colour. Nobody had ever said such a thing to her before, nor looked at her with just that kind of friendly interest. She shrugged, trying to pretend she wasn't bothered.

"I suppose so. I've never thought about it. We all talk like this in the valleys where I come from."

"In the *vall*-eys," he said, mimicking her, but there was no unkindness in his tone and he gave her a wide grin. "Well, I don't know what you're doing here slaving away for old Aggie, but if you ever need a friend Clarrie here'll tell you where to find me. Or Etty. They all know me round here, don't you, girls?"

"Only too well," Clarrie retorted, giving him a ferocious scowl, but he only laughed and swung out of the kitchen again, leaving his basket of bread behind.

"He's nice," Megan said. "Does he come here every day?"

"Oh, Tom's always in an' out," Clarrie said dismissively, as if he didn't matter in the least. "You don't want ter take no notice of 'im. Thinks a sight too much of 'imself, 'e does. Thinks 'e's God's gift to— Well, just you keep clear of 'im, that's all."

"Why? What's wrong with him?" Megan wanted to know, but Clarrie refused to say any more and it was left to Etty to explain later on, when Clarrie was out of the kitchen, helping to serve behind the bar.

"Clarrie likes Tom more than she lets on," she said shyly. "She'd like him to be her sweetheart. She don't like no other girl makin' up to 'im."

"I wasn't making up to him," Megan said, but she knew that Clarrie was the sort of girl who would be jealous of anyone who happened to be in the same room as the boy she was sweet on. "Well, it doesn't matter to me, anyway. I'm not going to be here long. And I'm not looking for a sweetheart." But she felt a little bit sorry all the same as she pictured Tom's open, cheerful face in her mind and thought of his offer of friendship. I need a friend, she thought, and I don't think I'm going to find many in this place.

But what could she do? There was no point in leaving, at least until she knew whether she could get news of her grandmother here. And meanwhile she was indoors out of the bitter cold, and getting food and drink of sorts and a roof over her head at night.

The thought of being cast out on to the streets again, alone, friendless, without even a halfpenny in her pocket, was more than she could bear.

Chapter 11

A week passed, with no news about Megan's grand mother. Nobody seemed to know about another tavern with "bell" in its name, and the man Aggie had promised might know Mrs Coleman never seemed to come in. Megan asked some of the other customers, but they all shook their heads, and after a day or two Aggie told her to stay in the kitchen and help Etty with washing-up and preparing food.

"Clarrie and Ruth can serve," she said. "They knows the customers an' they can give as good as they get. You're too shy an' quiet."

After that, Megan didn't have a chance to ask questions. She was shut in the kitchen all day and never saw anyone except for the tradesmen who called, like Tom Bradley the baker's son or Fred Wilmott the butcher's boy, or the rough-looking man who brought vegetables and always leered at her round the door.

There wasn't even much time to talk to them. She and Etty were kept busy all the time, scrubbing, peeling and washing. Betsy was at the table all day, mixing and rolling pastry for her pies, or squashing balls of suety dough into dumplings for the stew and chopping meat into lumps. There was a constant cloud of steam hanging in the air, and it was alternately hot and cold as the fire burned in the range, the cooking pots bubbled on the hob and tradesmen came and went, opening the door to let in a bitter blast of air.

"I've never knowed it so cold," Etty said, shivering. She was thinner and paler than ever, her skin almost transparent, and her cough seemed as if it would shake her frail body to bits. Sometimes she turned her head aside to spit phlegm into the waste-bucket, and once Megan noticed that it was speckled with red as if it were blood. She found herself feeling almost as anxious as if Etty were her own sister.

"It's a real cold snap," Betsy agreed. "They say the Serpentine's freezin' already. An' there's ice on the Thames."

Tom had just come in with a basket of warm, sweet-smelling bread. The scent of it always made Megan feel sick with hunger – all the servants were allowed was the stale bread left from yesterday. She longed to break a piece of crust from one of the loaves, but didn't dare.

"There'll be skating on the Serpentine soon, if it keeps up," he said cheerfully. "They're talking about ice fairs. That'll be something to see!"

"Ice fairs?" Megan said.

"That's right – skating, bands, hot chestnuts, fireworks, just like a real fair," he said, his eyes sparkling. "I'll take you to see it, shall I?"

Megan felt a warm blush of delight spread over her body, and she looked at him, opening her mouth to say yes, but at that moment the taproom door opened and Clarrie came in. She gave them a sharp look.

"Take 'er where?" she demanded.

Tom shrugged. "Nowhere much. I just thought of somewhere where she might find her gran, that's all. I'll need that basket back, Etty, if you want to take the bread out. We're a bit short today."

Etty and Megan swiftly emptied the basket and he slung it over his arm and opened the door. He glanced back and winked.

"See you tomorrow! And I'll try and find out a bit more about what we were talking about, Meggie, all right? I think it might be worth a try."

"All right," she said, blushing again, and turned away hastily to start slicing the warm bread. It would be served with the stew, or with cheese, with lots of pickled onions. The smell and feel of it was like torture.

Clarrie looked at her suspiciously as the door closed behind Tom.

"What was 'e on about? 'As 'e really found yer gran?"

"I don't know," Megan said, and to her relief the taproom door opened again and Aggie marched in, saving her from having to say any more. Clarrie was ordered sharply back to the taproom, where customers were shouting for more ale. She gave Megan another unbelieving look as she left.

71

Megan went on with her work, feeling miserable. She had come to London thinking that it would be easy to find her grandmother and enlist her help. Now she knew that it was much more difficult than she had supposed – that it might even be impossible.

What was she to do? She lay awake at night wondering what was happening at home to her mother and the little ones. Owen would look after them as best he could, she knew that, but he was working long hours in the pit, and came home too dog-tired to do anything more than swallow his supper and fall asleep. And how were they managing without her wage, pitiful though it was?

If only she could send some money home! But Aggie had paid her nothing so far, saying she was earning no more than her keep and anyway it was better for Aggie to keep her wages until she needed them. She thought of trying to find another place to work, but by now Etty and the others had told her dreadful stories of what London life was really like, and she was afraid to give up what she had for the world that lay outside.

"Hundreds of people sleep out in the streets," Etty said. "They got nowhere else to go, see. You can see 'em in doorways at night, all huddled up together to try an' keep warm. Some of 'em got no shoes and hardly any clothes, just a few rags. I bet there's a lot'll die in this cold weather."

"And if the cold don't get 'em, starvation will," Tom agreed. "They're nothing more than skeletons, some of 'em, living on other people's rubbish, and having to fight the rats for that. Sooner you find your gran the better, Meggie."

But what hope was there of finding her grandmother when she didn't know where she was? If only she hadn't lost her scrap of paper with the address on. If only she could remember the name of the inn.

Chapter 12

Ice covered the windows in the mornings, freezing the condensation of the night before into strange, wild patterns like forests of tropical trees. The Serpentine had frozen to a depth of thirteen inches, Tom said, and again he invited Megan to go with him to see the ice fair.

"Sunday afternoon. You get time off then, don't you?" The girls were all allowed a few hours off after Sunday dinner, when the inn closed until evening. "We'll go and see what it's all about."

Megan hesitated. Usually on Sunday afternoons she roamed the streets looking for another inn with "bell" in its name, coming back feeling even more hopeless.

She had grown to know Kensington quite well, even the Potteries district which was the most desperately poor place she had ever seen. Its roads were no better than rivers of mud, frozen now into great, rutted glaciers of ice. And the people who lived there were a motley crowd of rough, snarling creatures, barely human, who looked not much different from the animals they kept.

Megan had never expected to find animals in

London, other than horses. But in the Potteries it was like a farmyard, for they bred and trained pigs, game-cocks, bull-terriers and even rats – all for sport. Any animals that could run would be set against others in a race, while those who could fight were pitched in battles which generally ended in death. Inside the pot-houses were advertisements for these events: *Rat matches every Monday night* or *Cock-fighting here on Saturdays*. These fights and races took place behind the inns, or out in the road amongst all the black filth, the animal manure and running sewage that flowed down the gutters, often blocked into puddles of thick slime by dams of broken bottles, bricks or other debris.

The Potteries was a horrible place and Megan was almost thankful not to find her grandmother there.

Indeed, she had begun to despair of ever finding her grandmother. And although she knew that she ought to go on looking for her, the idea of wandering about alone yet again in the bitter cold made her feel ill.

"Come on," Tom urged her. "Come to the fair with me. It'll be fun."

Fun! Megan could scarcely remember the last time she had had fun. The only fair she had ever been to was a local one in the Rhondda, brought once a year by gypsies and cheap-jacks to a village a mile or two away from her own. Everyone enjoyed it, but that was because they all knew each other, had known each other all their lives. How could you have "fun" with strangers?

"You'll never see anything like it again," Tom said coaxingly. "It isn't every year the Serpentine freezes like this."

"All right," Megan said, making up her mind, "I'll come. To tell you the truth, I don't know where to look for Grandma next. I think I've been to every street in Kensington and nobody knows her, and there's no other inn with 'bell' in its name. I just don't know what to do."

Her voice broke a little and Tom stared at her. Then he moved closer and put his arm awkwardly round her shoulders.

"Meggie, don't cry. Look, I'll tell you what I'll do, I'll ask my old man if he knows any way we could find her. There must be some way – maybe someone's got a list of pubs in London, or something like that, and we could find her that way. I mean, there are street directories, aren't there? She'll be in one of those for certain."

"Street directories?" Megan asked doubtfully.

"Yes – books with every street listed in them, and all the people in all the houses. I dunno how you get hold of them, but there must be some way. My dad'll know. Tell you what – I'll ask him tonight, and then you can come round to our house for a bite to eat after we've been to the fair, and he'll tell you if he's found anything out."

"Oh Tom, would you really?" Megan looked up into his face. She wanted to throw her arms around his neck and kiss him, but at that moment the kitchen door opened and Betsy came in, followed by Etty who had gone to help her fetch water from the pump. And at the same time Clarrie came through from the taproom, her sharp eyes staring suspiciously.

"I told you to keep clear of Tom Bradley," she said to Megan after he had gone.

"I can't help it if he comes into the kitchen when I'm here, can I?" Megan retorted. She was getting tired of Clarrie treating Tom as if he were her property. He'd never shown any sign of liking her much, and if he chose to ask Megan to the ice fair that was his business. All the same, Megan knew that Clarrie could be very spiteful and wouldn't hesitate to make trouble for her if she thought Tom had chosen Megan as his "sweetheart", so she said nothing more and turned away.

In any case, I'm not his sweetheart, she thought. We're just going to the fair together. I don't even *want* a sweetheart. I just want to find Grandma and go home to help Mam.

All she wanted was a friend. And Tom was the only person, apart from Etty, who had shown her any real friendship.

Chapter 13

Sunday was bright, but still bitterly cold. In shady places, where the sun never reached, the frost lay in big glittering spikes as deep as snow. Trees and bushes were encrusted in a veil of diamond lace. There was ice right across the Thames now, and people were beginning to venture on to it with their skates, but the main crowd was still flocking to Hyde Park.

"They'll have ice fairs on the river after Christmas, if it stays as cold," Tom said, as he and Megan made their way towards the lake. Usually it was a dark, shimmering pool swarming with ducks and swans, and in the summer people could swim there, or hire little boats and row themselves about. But today there was no sign of a lake, just a vast sheet of glistening ice thronged with people who flocked around the stalls that had been set up.

"There's beautiful!" Megan said, stopping to gaze with delight at the colourful scene, and Tom laughed.

"I love the way you talk, Meggie, as if you're singing all the time. It's such a happy sound."

Megan shook her head ruefully. "I try to keep

cheerful, Tom, but it isn't easy, you know. So many things have happened to me." She hesitated. She had never told Tom just why she had come from Wales to look for her grandmother, but the friendly way he looked at her, the warmth in his eyes and the whiteness of his teeth when he smiled made her think that he would understand.

But there was no time now. Already they were approaching the edge of the frozen lake, where the first stalls had been set up and cheap-jacks were shouting, urging them to come and try their wares. Megan suddenly felt embarrassed; she had no money to buy fairings. But Tom took her hand and drew her gently on to the ice.

"Let's have a glass of punch to warm us up," he suggested. "And it's my treat. I've been saving up for a day like this!"

Megan hesitated for no more than a moment. One glance at his laughing face told her that he meant it. He had invited her to come because he wanted her company, and all she had to do was enjoy it.

And why not? Hadn't she had enough misery during the past year? Wasn't it time she had a little pleasure?

The stalls were set up around the edge of the big lake, leaving the centre clear for skating, dancing and band concerts. Tom had skates, and Megan watched admiringly as he put them on and swooped away from her. He flew across the ice, his long scarf fluttering behind him, and when he came back his face was glowing.

"You try. We can hire skates over there."

Megan shrank away. "Oh, I couldn't, I'd fall." But Tom laughed and coaxed her on to the ice with him, and when she teetered gingerly away from the man who was loaning skates, he held her arm firmly and kept her upright.

"It's easy. Just hold my hands and let yourself go." Holding both her hands in his, he skated backwards, drawing her along with him. For a few minutes Megan was stiff with tension, then she relaxed suddenly, feeling the blades cut into the ice, and her feet glided smoothly across the shining surface.

"Oh, it's lovely!" she cried, and her cheeks flushed with pink, partly pleasure and partly cold. But she couldn't feel really cold with Tom's warm hands enclosing hers and his bright-blue eyes smiling into her face. She laughed back at him and he gripped her hands more tightly, twirled on his skates so that he was beside her, and slipped his arm round her waist.

Holding her close, he began to skate in time to the music being played by the band. Megan drew in a gasp of panic, but once again she knew she couldn't fall with Tom holding her so securely, and she held his hand against her waist, keeping her other hand closely in his, and let the music guide her steps.

"It's like magic," she whispered. "We're flying!"

Tom chuckled. "It's as near as you can get to it," he agreed. "Megan, you're a natural skater. Can you dance as well on ordinary ground?"

Megan thought of days in the valleys, when they had taken time off from the grinding toil of the pits for a celebration – a wedding, perhaps, or Christmas. Her mother had been a fine dancer once, knowing all the old Welsh melodies, and she had taught Megan the clog-dancing which was so peculiarly graceful in thick, heavy shoes.

"I used to love it," she said a little sadly, for the dancing days seemed long past now. Mam hadn't lifted a step in gaiety since Dadda had died, and her clogs had been pushed to the back of a cupboard, or just used for working.

They took her skates back reluctantly, and then walked around the rest of the fair. At the edge of the lake, sand had been spread on the ice to make it easier to walk on, and there were hot-chestnut sellers, baked potato stalls, tents where you could buy drinks of all kinds, hot or cold, and charcoal braziers where you could just gather to warm yourself.

As the early winter darkness fell, the Serpentine looked even more magical, with the stallholders lighting lamps and torches. People came and went, their faces showing brightly for a moment in the lamplight then fading into the darkness, or obscured by the drifting smoke of the many lamps and fires. They gathered round the booths, showing off their skills with the shotguns or shying wooden balls at coconuts, and Tom won a tiny, bright-eyed wooden doll which he presented to Megan with a flourish.

"Oh *Tom*!" Megan had never had a real doll in her life. Dadda had made her one once out of sticks and a few rags, and he'd drawn a smiling face on it, but it hadn't been like this one. She held the little toy tightly, slipping it into her pocket for safe keeping. "*Thank* you."

They walked right round the fair and on past it, to where the ice glimmered in darkness under a rising moon. It was more slippery here, with no sand, and Tom clasped Megan's hand in his to prevent her from falling. They looked at the lights of the city twinkling in the frosty air, and watched with delight as fireworks soared into the sky, bursting in a shower of coloured stars.

"It looks so pretty," Megan said softly. "Like fairyland. It's hard to believe there are dark narrow streets there, full of dirt and rubbish, and people sleeping in doorways and freezing to death. And starving children with only a few rags and no shoes." She shivered. "They say it's like living at the end of the rainbow, but it's a cruel place, London is."

"Life *is* cruel," Tom said quietly. "You don't have to be in London to find that out."

Megan thought about the skip falling suddenly into the mine, burying the men at the bottom of the shaft with coal. Tom was right. There was sadness everywhere, not just in London.

But there was happiness too. There was skating on the Serpentine on a bright winter's day, and there were people like Tom, full of friendship and warmth.

And there had been dancing for her mother, and happiness with Dadda, and the comfort of family life.

I'll give it back to her, she thought with sudden determination. I'll give her back that happiness. Somehow, I'll get her away from Morgan Jones.

They were almost back at the fair. The light of the torches flared out across the ice, bringing a glow like sunset to the faces of the people who gathered around the stalls. Megan looked at them, and then stiffened and gave a little cry.

"What is it?" Tom tightened his hand as if to stop her falling. "What's the matter?"

"That man – see, the one with the tall hat and the grey beard." Megan pointed eagerly. "It's Mr Coleman, I'm sure it is – Mr Coleman, who married Grandma. And look – the woman with him – it's *her*! It's my *grandma*! They're here, Tom, they're *here* – oh, catch them, we must catch them. *Don't let them get away!*"

Chapter 14

Filled with excitement, Megan pulled herself away from Tom and ran forwards, her arms outstretched. But she had forgotten the ice. The next moment, she slipped and fell with a little scream of pain.

People nearby gathered round immediately, and Tom pushed through the crowd and bent over her anxiously. She was already trying to get up, but her leg was twisted beneath her and she sank back with a little moan of pain and gazed at him beseechingly.

"Grandma – find Grandma for me, Tom. Don't let her disappear."

He glanced over to the booth where Megan had seen the man and woman, but they had vanished. He couldn't follow without leaving Megan alone on the ice. He bent over her again.

"Where does it hurt, Meggie? What have you done?"

"It's just my ankle – I've twisted it, that's all." She tried to get up again but the pain showed in her face. "Please, Tom, go after Grandma."

"I can't, Meggie. She's already gone. I'd never find them now, in the dark and all this crowd. And I can't leave you here."

He lifted her in his arms. She was as light as a feather, her slender body like a bird's in his arms. He carried her to the edge of the ice and sat her on the grass. The crowd had lost interest now that it was obvious she wasn't badly hurt, and drifted away.

"Oh, Tom," she sobbed, "just as I was about to find her! It's not fair!"

"Never mind," he soothed her. "At least you've seen her. You know she's in London. We'll find her again, Meggie, never fear. I'll help you to find her." He looked around. "What we've got to do now is get you back home. You can't walk all that way."

"And you can't carry me," she said miserably. "What are we going to do?"

"I can carry you to the edge of the park," Tom said decisively. "And then we'll hire a hansom cab to take us home. I've got just enough money for that."

He lifted Megan in his arms again and carried her to the road. All the way, Megan kept looking into the faces of the passers-by in the hope of seeing her grandmother again, but there was no sign of her. It was almost as if she had imagined that kindly face under the curling grey hair. But I didn't imagine it, she told herself fiercely. I did see her, I *did*.

When they reached the road, Tom set her down again. She stood beside him, leaning on his shoulder, keeping her injured foot off the ground. Whenever she let it touch anything, a red-hot pain shot through her ankle.

"I won't be able to stand on it for days. What's

Aggie going to say? She'll push me out."

"She won't. She'll just give you a stool to sit on while you work." Tom spoke grimly. "There aren't all that many girls like you, willing to work all hours for nothing more than a hunk of stale bread and a bowl of leftover soup. Aggie Crowther treats her servants worse than the workhouse. I've wondered many a time why any of you stay."

Megan said nothing. She knew why the other girls stayed: Etty, because she was too frail and sickly to look for another job, Ruth because she was too simple to think of it, and Clarrie – well, the reason why Clarrie stayed was because she had set her cap at Tom and wanted to stay where she could see him every day. Besides, there were too few jobs to be had and too many cold and starving people already on the streets for anyone to risk joining them.

As for Megan herself, what else could she do? Who else would take her in and give her a roof and just enough food to keep her alive while she searched for her grandmother?

"Why is it so important to you to find her?" Tom asked gently. "I've looked at you many a time and wondered just why you came to London. What drove you away from the valleys, Megan? What happened to you, back in Wales?"

The evening air was growing colder. A few hansom cabs clopped by, but they were all taken. Megan shivered and drew her shawl closer around her shoulders. Tom put his arm around her again, holding her against the warmth of his body, and she started to tell him her story, all about Mam and Morgan Jones, and the day that Dadda died in the pit.

"And so, you see, I've got to find Grandma. She's the only one who can help. And I know she would, if she only knew what was happening."

"But why hasn't she ever written to you?" Tom asked, frowning. "And you say your mam wrote to her when your father died. Why didn't she answer?"

Megan shrugged. "I don't know. But since I've come to London, I've wondered – was the address we had for her wrong in some way? I haven't found any-one who knows her in Kensington, nor the inn she runs. And there's something else I've thought of."

"What's that?" he asked.

"Well, suppose Grandma can't read or write? Mam can't. Owen or me, we wrote the letters she sent Grandma. Dadda could write a little, but not much. Owen and me, we learnt at the school we went to, but we were only there a little while. I don't remember ever seeing Grandma read when she lived in the village, but there was nothing to read anyway. We don't have many newspapers and nobody has books or anything like that."

Tom looked thoughtful. "You may be right. But her new husband – Mr Coleman – *he* must be able to read and write. He runs an inn. He must be able to do the business."

An empty cab came along just then and Tom hailed it with relief. He was getting worried about keeping

Megan out in the bitter cold. It was well below freezing now, and the air itself seemed to bite your skin. He'd heard of people's ears dropping off, or their noses going rotten with the cold, and he could feel the pain in his own fingers and toes.

He gave the driver the address of his father's bake-house and helped Megan climb up into the cab. They sat together, huddling close for warmth, as the horse clip-clopped its way through the frozen streets.

Once away from the merrymaking in Hyde Park, London began to show its darker face, the one that Megan had called cruel. The narrower streets were mean and dirty, ill-lit alleyways of creeping shadows and sinister menace. Old women shuffled out of doorways, bent old men tapped their sticks along the edge of the gutters, and children scurried like rats along the walls. Sometimes the light of a gas-lamp shone briefly on a boy or girl, and Megan thought they looked like gnomes or goblins, wizened old faces on stunted bodies.

She had thought that it would be too cold for people to be out now, but to her surprise the main streets were crowded. Taverns spilled light out on to the pavements when their doors were opened; beggars clustered around the gas-lamps, holding out claw-like hands in entreaty; men and youths lounged together in surly groups. It was like the opposite of the ice carnival – a fair of misery, a gathering of people who had come together to share their despair.

"They've got nothing to keep them warm at home," Tom said. "They live in hovels and tenements – the old mansion houses that were built a hundred years ago, or more. They're falling down now and these people live in them like rats in holes. They're damp and rotten and nobody dares light a fire because most of them don't have fireplaces and the whole lot might go up in smoke, so they have to come out to the taverns to keep warm. Or they go to the ones who do have fireplaces and share their fire, and do their bit of cooking – if they've got anything to cook."

Megan gazed out of the cab window in horror. Even though there were so many people, there was a strange, frightening silence. The faces of the crowd were grey, their eyes dull. It was as if they had no hope of anything better, as if they were just waiting for fate to work its own plan.

"But they all look half-starved. Doesn't *anyone* have enough to eat in London?"

"Oh yes, some do. But there are thousands like these. They pick up a bit of work here and there, labouring or holding horses. Or they work on the railways – the new underground railway is giving quite a few jobs. But it's too cold for that sort of work now. The ground's frozen too hard, and nobody can do anything outside. So there's no wages."

Megan felt the cold seep into her own bones, even though she was still sitting close to Tom, warmed by his body. She was not surprised that people were starving. If you couldn't work, you had no money, and if you had no money, you had no food – it was as simple as that. And soon you had nowhere to live, and just had to sleep in the streets and the draughty doorways, as so many desperate people were doing now.

You could go to the workhouse – she had seen the one in Kensington, a big, grim building with hundreds of small barred windows like a prison – but there were so many people clamouring for relief now that the workhouse itself was forced to turn them away. Instead, the wardens handed out bread, but even then there wasn't enough for the throng which increased daily, and the stronger ones pushed to the front of the crowd and snatched what there was, while the weak trudged hopelessly away.

The cab had arrived in Kensington. It was close to the street where Tom's father had his bakehouse when Megan felt Tom draw in a quick, sharp breath of dismay.

Like so many others they had passed through, the street was full of people. But these were not silent; they were angry, their faces dark and distorted as they stampeded along the narrow pavement, blocking the road, waving sticks and cudgels, and they were bawling and swearing, their voices cracked and rusty with a despair that had turned to hatred.

"Tom!" Megan gasped. "What is it? What's happening?"

"It's a bread riot," Tom said, grimly. "I've heard of it happening in other parts of London. They're crying out for bread, Meggie. They've gone mad with hunger and they're attacking the bakehouses."

Chapter 15

The cab driver stopped his horse abruptly and tapped on the roof with his whip.

"I ain't goin' down there, mate. You better give me yer fare now. I don't want to get mixed up in no trouble."

Tom felt in his pocket and pulled out a few coins. He passed them up to the driver and helped Megan from the cab. She put her foot to the ground and felt the stab of pain.

"I don't think I can walk, Tom."

He supported her with one arm around her waist and they shuffled to the corner, where she could lean against the wall. She looked at him with frightened eyes.

So far, the crowd had ignored them. They were all heading for the narrow street where the Bradleys' bakehouse stood, but they were moving slowly, for there were other shops along the way and they seemed determined to loot every one.

Megan could see people at upper windows, leaning out, shouting at the mob to go away. But no one took any notice. The shop doors were firmly closed, but already men were battering at them as if determined to force their way in. They came to a smaller bakehouse which stood in the main street and stood outside, chanting furiously.

"Bread! Bread! Bread! Give us bread! Bread! *Bread!*"

"We're starvin' ter death!" someone yelled above the chanting. "We got to 'ave bread. There ain't nothin' else. Give us some bread, for Gawd's sake!"

The shouting paused, and the baker's voice could be heard in reply. "But there isn't any. We've sold all we made today, and the new batch isn't ready yet. You'll have to wait till morning—"

"Don't believe 'im!" someone called out. "They've got bread in there now, I can smell it! Smash down that door and let's get at it."

"We haven't got bread. It's the dough you can smell, the dough and the yeast. It takes all night to bake—" The man's voice was lost in the roar of rage. The crowd made a rush for the house and the door shuddered. Even the walls seemed to shake.

Megan felt sick with fear. The crowd didn't sound like human beings any more, they sounded like animals, or rather one huge, ferocious animal that had been let loose from some foreign jungle. Talking to them wouldn't make any difference, she knew that. They couldn't hear ordinary voices any more. They could only hear the roar of their own blood, the rumbling of their own empty stomachs, the fury of their own desperation.

"I'll have to fetch help," Tom said to her. "I'll have

to find a constable. But I can't leave you here…"

She looked up at him. She was terrified, but she knew that he was right. If someone didn't come soon, the crowd would smash their way into the bakehouse and then there was no knowing what might happen. And it could only be a short time before they found the bigger Bradley bakehouse.

"I'll be all right. I'll hide in this doorway. They won't see me."

"I hate leaving you," he said. "You can't even run away."

"I'll be all right," she said again, and gave him a push. "Go on – but don't be too long, will you?"

He gave her a brief smile and touched her cheek with his finger. "I'll be back before you know I've gone," he said, and vanished into the darkness.

Megan watched him go. She crouched in the corner, feeling suddenly desperately lonely. The crowd surged around her, passing her without a glance, but the miasma of their animal fury wrapped itself about her like a cobweb of evil, clinging to her trembling skin and soaking into her bones. An icy wind bit through her shawl and she shivered, as cold as if she were naked.

"Bread!" the crowd yelled, and now it was like a howl, the howl of some ravenous and predatory animal. "Give us bread! Bread, bread *bread*!"

There were women among them, young women with babies in their arms, old women almost too stiff and twisted to move. They all had the same desperate expression on their faces, the contorting, overpowering hunger of people who have not eaten properly for weeks, for months, perhaps never in their whole lives. Nothing mattered to them now but the relief of that terrible grinding emptiness, nothing but the simplest, most basic kind of food to fill their starving bellies — bread.

Megan remembered her father telling her about the riots in Merthyr Tydfil thirty years before. Twenty people had been killed, over sixty hurt, and the ringleaders had been hanged at Cardiff jail. He had been taken to see them as a little boy, rotting and swinging in their gibbets, and he had never forgotten it.

Suppose people were killed here tonight, in this narrow London street. Could Tom bring help in time to prevent it?

Chapter 16

The waiting seemed endless. Huddled in her corner as the crowd swirled and surged around the little street, Megan felt almost as if her blood were freezing in her veins. Her head ached with the bitter cold, her fingers and toes were numb, and the pain in her ankle had turned into a dull, agonizing throb. And all the time she was afraid that someone would notice her there and drag her out, or attack her simply because she was alone and helpless.

"Bread!" The chant went on, on, on. "Bread, bread *bread…*"

They were still hammering at the door, still trying to break it down, but the baker had had a stout new door fitted quite recently, and had reinforced it when he began to expect trouble. All the same, it couldn't hold out for ever and already some of them were beginning to move on, in the direction of the cul-de-sac where the Bradleys lived.

If only she could *do* something, even let Mr Bradley know that he was in danger, but help was on its way. If she could get to the bakehouse…

Was there a back way?

The street was a cul-de-sac. The only way to the back of the bakehouse, which stood across the end, was through an alleyway from the next street. That meant coming out of her dark corner, going along the main street, down the next and round the back to the alley.

I can't, Megan thought. I'd never get there. Even if I could walk properly, someone would stop me.

Cautiously, she put her foot to the ground. The dull throbbing swelled to a shaft of vicious pain, and she almost cried out. But if she leant against the wall, she could ease herself along without putting too much pressure on it. And anything was better than just crouching in the corner, shivering with cold and terror, waiting for Tom to come back.

Very slowly, Megan dragged herself along the wall. To her relief, it got easier instead of harder. The pain stabbed her really badly if she put her foot down in a certain way, but by avoiding that she could keep it at a tolerable level. And having to stay close to the wall meant that she also stayed out of the glimmering light of the gas-lamps. She was no more than a shadow, melting into the darkness of the walls.

It seemed an eternity before she was out of the main street and creeping down the side street that ran parallel to the cul-de-sac. She was no longer cold; the effort brought sweat pouring down her face, and the pain was increasing now, her ankle protesting every time her foot touched the ground. I don't know how much further I can go, she thought.

But over the houses, she could still hear the sounds of the rioting. And it was moving, getting closer to the Bradleys' bakehouse. She had to warn Tom's father about what was happening. She had to make sure they weren't taken by surprise.

Where was Tom?

Megan came to the end of the street. She turned the corner. It was only a few yards to the alleyway. Once there, she could crawl on her hands and knees if necessary to reach the back door of the bakehouse.

Her ankle throbbed almost unbearably and she set her teeth, determined not to give in. A thin grey cat ran across in front of her, making her jump. Or was it a rat? She thought of the people with nowhere to go, sleeping on the streets, freezing and starving to death in doorways, and she thought of rats crawling over their bodies, sniffing, nibbling...

The alleyway stretched into darkness. Only one dim gas-lamp stood at its entrance; beyond that, it was a murky tunnel of evil smells and small, unpleasant sounds – a steady dripping here, a furtive scrabbling there. Megan leaned against the wall, peering down it, trying to pierce the gloom, but it was almost solid. She felt as if the darkness itself were a wall through which nothing could pass.

I can't go down there, she thought. *Anything* might be lurking in those shadows. And fearful visions, born half of the old tales of the Welsh mountains and half of the creeping terror that stalked the streets of London, came slithering into her mind, and her body turned cold again with horror.

But the sound of the rioters, coming faintly over the rooftops like the distant roar of wild animals, reminded her of the danger that Tom's parents were in. If they were working in their bakehouse, they might be unable to hear what was going on outside. With the doors unlocked and unbarricaded, they could be taken by surprise and find the rioters upon them before they knew anything about it.

Taking a deep breath, Megan forced herself to enter the alleyway. And less than a second later, the scream that had been lurking in her throat all this time broke from her lips as a large, heavy hand descended on her shoulder.

"And what do you think you're doin', wanderin' down a place like this all by yourself at this hour of the night?" a deep, gravelly voice growled in her ear. "Don't yer know it's dangerous for young ladies to be out all by themselves...?"

Chapter 17

"*Let* me go!" Frantic with terror, Megan tried to twist away from the hand which held her so mercilessly. "Let me go – *please,* let me go!"

"Not till I'm good and ready." She felt herself dragged deeper into the alley and closed her eyes, shaking with fear. "Now then – let's 'ave a look at yer."

"Please—" She opened her eyes again and realized that he had not dragged her further into the alley, but out into the dim glow of the gas-lamp. She stared at him in astonishment, her eyes moving over his dark blue swallow-tail coat and tall top hat.

"You're a policeman!"

"An' lucky for you I am," he said sternly. "I coulda bin any rapscallion out for easy pickin's." He looked at her more closely. "Here, I know you, don't I? You bin workin' for old Aggie Crowther. I thought you looked a decent young woman. What yer doin' 'ere, wanderin' about all on your tod? You'll get more than you bargain for one o' these fine nights."

"I'm not wandering about," Megan said. "I'm trying to get to Mr Bradley's bakehouse, to warn him.

There are rioters coming down the street, attacking the bakehouses. Tom Bradley's gone to fetch help."

"Rioters!" he said. "I thought I could hear a lotta noise. Well, it's bin boilin' up for the past coupla weeks, people out on the streets, beggin' for money and food, and nobody got enough to give 'em. Pitiful, it is. But you can't let 'em take the law into their own 'ands, all the same."

"Please," Megan said, "can't you help? Stop them, somehow? Or tell Mr Bradley so that they don't break in and do some terrible damage?"

"You need 'orses to stop a riot," the constable said. "That's who they'll send, the blokes on 'orses. But I'll tell yer what I'll do – I'll go in the back way through the bakehouse and 'ead 'em off a bit." He patted the wooden rattle that hung at his belt. "This'll give 'em something to think about. They'll think there's a 'ole platoon of us, see."

He dived back into the alleyway, with Megan at his heels. Pain or no pain, she wasn't going to be left alone again. Reaching out blindly, she caught at the tails of his coat and hung on determinedly, hobbling in his wake.

The bakehouse door was unlocked. The constable pushed it open and a cloud of steam billowed out. He pulled Megan inside with him and she let go of his coat and leaned against the door, too exhausted to move another inch.

The bakehouse was warm, already busy with its night's work, the air tingling with a fine dust of wheat-flour. Several boys and men were pulling out the first batch of loaves, crusty and fragrant, and loading the hot ovens with fresh trays. Tom Bradley's father was standing at a long wooden table, kneading dough, his sleeves rolled up over muscular arms. He looked round in surprise.

"What's all this? What's going on?"

"It's all right, Mr Bradley," the constable said quickly. "There's nothing amiss in here. But this young lady 'ere 'as given me certain information which I think you oughter be apprised of—"

"Cut the cackle," the baker interrupted. "You learn too many long words, you coppers. You never talked like that when we ran the streets together as nippers, Fred Bowling."

The policeman flushed and looked as if he'd like to arrest Mr Bradley for impertinence. But there was no time for that. The rioters could be heard outside, coming closer. He seized his rattle and headed for the front of the bakehouse.

"Oi! Where d'you think you're going?" The baker dropped his dough and made to follow him.

"It's a bread riot," Megan told him breathlessly. "They're coming down the street, a huge crowd of them. Tom's gone to fetch help – the policeman says they'll bring horses. But he's going to try to frighten them off with his rattle."

"With his *rattle*? For Gawd's sake – they're not a bunch of bloomin' babies!" Mr Bradley started after the policeman again. "Here, Fred Bowling, you come back this minute. I don't want your blood all over the shop, spoiling the bread. Leave 'em to me."

He jerked open the front door. The noise of the crowd suddenly swelled and, peering past him, Megan saw that they had started to come down the cul-de-sac. The light shone from the door and she saw the expressions on the faces of those in front, and shuddered. They caught sight of Mr Bradley and a howl went up like that of a pack of hounds scenting its quarry.

"Shut the door!" she cried in an agony of fear. "Oh, please, please, shut the door!"

Mr Bradley slammed it quickly. He put up a heavy chain and slid a solid bar of wood across. He leant his back against it and looked at Megan and the constable. He was breathing hard.

"They're like a lynch mob," he said in a wondering tone. "They're out for murder."

"They want bread," Megan said. "They're hungry."

The baker looked at her helplessly.

"But I'm *making* bread. It won't do them any good to come breaking in here. It'll be on the streets by dawn."

"I don't think they can wait till dawn," Megan said. "They're not just hungry, see – they're starving. And freezing. They're mad with it."

The two men looked at her. The rest of the workers had stopped and were staring with frightened eyes. One of them barred the back door as well.

"You sound as if you know," Mr Bradley said at last.

"Who are you? Where d'you come from?"

"I'm Megan Price." She spoke proudly. "I come from Wales. I've been to the ice fair with Tom."

"Tom? *My* Tom, you mean?" He stared at her. "Ah – now I know. You're the new girl working for Aggie Crowther. He's talked about you. Looking for your gran. So it's my Tom who's gone to fetch help, is it? Well, it ought to be along soon." He gave Megan a sharp look. "Here, you're white as a ghost. What's been happening to you?"

Megan shook her head. She couldn't start explaining now, about the pits and her father's death, about Morgan Jones and her desperate bid for help. Her ankle was throbbing badly and she felt suddenly sick. There was a roaring noise in her head, and as she looked back at the two men they seemed to blur and begin to spin slowly before her eyes. Round and round they went in a huge, dizzying circle, and then there was a sudden jerk and they were back in their proper positions, only to start again – and again – and again... And all the time she could hear Mr Bradley's last few words repeated over and over again – "*happening to you ... happening to you ... happening to you...*"

"Catch her, quick," someone said in a faint, far-away voice, and she wondered who it was, and who had to be caught and why. And then the spinning picture of the room darkened and she could see and hear no more.

Chapter 18

"That's it. Lay her down comfortable, and put this cushion under her head."

Megan lay quite still, her eyes still closed. She had no idea where she was and could remember nothing, only a crazy turmoil of angry faces and a tumult of shouting. The voice was quite unfamiliar, and yet after the first moment or two she felt sure she had heard it somewhere before. Recently. Perhaps only a few minutes ago.

She opened her eyes. Mr Bradley and the policeman were staring down at her. They had laid her on the floor, on a pile of sacking. The dust in it made her sneeze suddenly, and the men laughed with relief.

"That's the ticket," Mr Bradley said approvingly. "Passed out for a minute or two, didn't you. How you feeling now? Think a sip o' water'd do any good?"

Megan nodded weakly. The policeman helped her sit up and Mr Bradley held a cup of water to her lips. Outside, she heard a noise like thunder, and the big front door shook. She looked at them with sudden fear.

"It's all right," Tom's father said comfortingly. "They won't bust that down in a hurry."

"But—"

"You said my Tom was on the way with horses. He'll be here any minute, and that'll make short shrift of 'em. Mind, I'm sorry for them, but what can I do? I got a living to earn, and it's those who order and pay for the bread that'll get it."

Having made sure that Megan was not about to die, the policeman went to the back door again. She could hear him out in the alleyway, energetically swinging his rattle. It made a fearsome clattering that would be heard for several streets, and any policeman within range would instantly come to help.

"I dunno why they use those rattles," Mr Bradley said. "A good whistle'd be better." He glanced a little anxiously at the door. There was a steady thudding on the other side, as if people were throwing themselves against it, and it was beginning to shake. "I think we'd better go upstairs."

Megan started to get to her feet and then fell back with a little cry. For a few moments, she had forgotten all about her injured ankle. Mr Bradley looked at her with concern and she gave him a rueful smile.

"I twisted it on the ice. Tom brought me back in a hansom cab."

He shook his head and helped her to her feet, then supported her up the stairs. The other workers were already there, with Mr Bradley's wife and Tom's sister Enid, all sitting on sacks of flour.

"We'll be safer up here," Mr Bradley said, and he went to the wooden doorway which opened above the street, where the flour was delivered from the wagons. There was a small hatchway in the door and he opened it and peered out. "They're an ugly-looking mob."

As soon as the hatch was opened the shouts flooded into the room. "*Bread – bread – bread –*" and continued until someone noticed the baker looking down at them. The noise rose to a bellow, then there were shouts for silence and slowly the crowd quietened, until only one voice could be heard.

"Open up, baker! We want bread, an' we're not waitin' no longer."

"That's right," a chorus of voices joined in. "Open up an' let us 'ave what should be ours."

Mr Bradley waited until silence fell again and then he called down to them, his voice strong and calm.

"I'm sorry, I know what you're feeling." There were jeers and catcalls at this, cries of "How can you know? Your belly's always full", and he waited again, then went on, "If I could feed you all, I would. But there's not enough flour in the place, and even if there were I can't take bread away from my regular customers. Look, why don't you go round to the workhouse? It's their job to help you and they've got their own bakehouse there—"

At this suggestion, a howl of rage went up that surpassed any noise the crowd had made until now. The door was suddenly peppered by a hail of stones and broken bottles, and Mr Bradley drew in his head hastily and shut the hatch. He was pale.

"They've been to the workhouse," Megan said

quietly. "They haven't got enough themselves. People are coming away empty-handed day after day."

"It's terrible," Mrs Bradley said. "It's like a famine."

They heard heavy footsteps on the stairs and the constable appeared. He was breathing heavily.

"I've called for assistance," he said. "Reinforcements should be arrivin' at any moment."

"Well, thank the Lord for that," Mr Bradley said. "But what are you going to do in the meantime? It's your job to control that mob out there. If they go on battering at my door like that they'll smash it to bits and be in here, and *then* what'll you do, eh? Tell me that!"

The policeman was saved from answering by a sudden increase in the noise. But it wasn't just shouting that came to the ears of the listeners in the bakehouse now. Lifting her head, Megan could hear other sounds – the clatter of more policemen's rattles, and the welcome sound of horses' hooves.

The crowd fell suddenly silent. The barrage of missiles against the door ceased.

Cautiously, Mr Bradley went to the hatchway and opened it again. He peered out, taking care not to show himself more than he had to. Then he beckoned to the others.

The policeman was there first, bustling forward importantly. He almost shoved Mr Bradley aside in his eagerness to see. The baker glared at him and pushed back, and the constable staggered a little and looked daggers.

"Let the wife see," Mr Bradley said. "And the girls."

"I don't know as that's safe—"

"Come over here, Joan," the baker said, ignoring him. "Look at this. In our little street!"

Mrs Bradley and her daughter went over to stand by his side. They looked down and gasped.

Megan pulled herself off her sack and hobbled across the floor. She leaned against the wall and peered over Enid's shoulder and down through the little square hatchway.

The mob was quite silent. It had turned as one man, away from the bakehouse, to face towards the end of the cul-de-sac – the only way out. And that way was barred by a line of huge black horses, each ridden by a policeman in a dark, flowing coat and tall hat that made them look at least thirteen or fourteen feet above the ground.

And at the front of the line of horses, facing the crowd, stood Tom.

As Megan stared down, he glanced up and gazed straight at her. She saw his mouth move, as if he were saying her name. He grinned, his teeth gleaming white even at that distance, and he took off his cap and waved it three times in the air.

As if at a prearranged signal, the mob charged.

what happened next?

"Where did Tom go?" she asked urgently. "Where is he?"

Mr Bradley turned and looked at her in surprise.

"Tom? I dunno where he went. You said he'd gone off to fetch help; it muster been him called this lot out. Look at *that*!"

One of the horses had fallen. It was on its knees, the police rider flung from its back as it toppled sideways. The crowd drew back for a moment, then pressed forward, keeping a wary eye on the deadly hooves.

"But he was there," Megan said. "Do you mean to say you never saw him? He was in front of the horses – he waved his cap."

"That chap? That was *Tom*?"

"Yes."

Mr Bradley stared at her for a moment. Then he sat down heavily on one of the sacks of flour, and rubbed his hand over his face.

"I never realized – I never *saw* him, not properly. Our Tom! No wonder the missus was so upset." He took his hand away and stared at her again. "You *sure* about that?"

"Yes," Megan said, wishing miserably that she could say no. But it had definitely been Tom. He had seen her. Smiled at her. Waved. And because of that, perhaps he was now lying, crushed and broken, beneath a storm of trampling feet…

Oh *Tom*…

Chapter 20

The battle was beginning to lessen. The people nearest the entrance to the cul-de-sac had escaped and taken to their heels. Suddenly the street was almost empty, apart from the stamping horses and a few men and women who had been knocked over and were slowly getting to their feet.

"It's a miracle," Megan said, staring down. "Nobody's been killed. I thought..." Her voice trembled and broke. "But where's Tom?"

"Here I am," said a cheerful voice behind her, and she whirled round to see his familiar face grinning at her as if nothing had happened.

"*Tom!* But how – where – what *happened* to you?" She flung herself into his arms, half-sobbing with relief, then drew back. "Look at you. You're covered in mud – and your jacket's torn – and you've lost your cap!"

"It's all right," he said, laughing. "I've got another cap." He turned to his mother, who was still crouched on the pile of sacks, shaking with distress. "Don't cry, Ma. It's all over now. I'm safe. And they won't come back." His face sobered. "It's all wrong, though –

having to get the police to chase people off just because they're hungry. They're not criminals, those people – they're just starving."

"All the same," the policeman said, "we can't let 'em just run riot in the streets. It won't do no good to break into places and smash everything up. That's not going to 'elp anyone. None of us'll 'ave any bread then."

He pulled his swallow-tailed coat around him and picked up his top hat, which he'd taken off to come up the stairs. "I shall 'ave to go back to the station and make my report," he said. "I may want to talk to you again, young Tom. And the young lady 'ere. You're important witnesses."

He went off down the stairs and Mr Bradley shook his head and sighed. "I dunno. You're right, Tom, they're not criminals, they're just ordinary people that want to work and feed their families, and what with this terrible cold and all, they can't do either. It's a terrible thing to have to watch your children starve and know you can't do anything about it."

Mrs Bradley had stopped crying and sat up. She was holding her son's hand tightly, as if she was afraid to let him go again, and Enid was sitting close to her other side. Megan looked at them and felt a sharp stab of homesickness. They were a family and, no matter how welcoming and kind they were, she was on the outside. She longed for Mam and Owen, and Dafydd and the little ones.

Tom met her eyes. He gave her a smile – not a grin

this time, but a real smile which told her that he hadn't forgotten her, and that he knew what she was feeling.

"I hope you've got some supper cooking," he said to his mother. "I promised Meggie something to warm her up after we'd been to the ice fair."

"Supper!" Mrs Bradley exclaimed. "Why, it'll be burned to a frazzle!"

She jumped up and ran down the stairs and everyone else moved at the same moment. The baker's men went back to attend to their dough and their ovens, and Mr Bradley hurried down to oversee them. Enid followed her mother, and Tom gave Megan his usual friendly grin.

"Well, that's that bit of excitement over," he remarked. "I hope you weren't too frightened, Meggie. I can tell you, when I got back and found you weren't where I'd left you, I was scared stiff. I thought someone'd run off with you!"

"You shouldn't have thought that," she said shyly, and he laughed.

"Well, I knew you couldn't run off by yourself! How did you get up here?"

"I managed to get round to the back. The policeman helped me. I was afraid they'd break in before you got back. I had to warn your father." She tried to get up and grimaced.

"Your foot's still bad, isn't it. Let me look." He bent and Megan lifted the hem of her skirt so that he could see her foot, encased in the thick clogs she'd always worn at the pit. Tom gave a low whistle.

"No wonder it hurts! It's swollen up like a balloon. Look at the bruise. It's like a rainbow."

Megan peered down. Her ankle was puffy, and turning a dark blue. She stared at it in dismay.

"What am I going to do?"

"You're going to rest it," Tom said decisively. "That ankle's got to be looked after. No walking, no running and no standing until it's better."

"But Mrs Crowther – she won't keep me if I can't work. She'll throw me out. I'll be like those poor people out there, with nowhere to sleep, nothing to eat—"

"You won't," he said firmly. "I won't let you. Anyway, didn't I tell you Aggie would just give you a stool and tell you to get on with it?" There was a call from downstairs. "Supper's ready. You'll feel better with something hot inside you. Ma's stews are as good as old Betsy Smith's are, any day. And we'll ask Dad if he's got any ideas about how to find your gran."

Grandma! Megan had almost forgotten about her. She turned to Tom, her eyes bright with hope.

"Do you think he'll be able to help? Oh Tom, suppose that *was* her we saw at the fair. She must be in London somewhere." Her shoulders sagged. "But it's such an enormous place. I never realized how big it was till I came here…"

"Let's go down and have supper," he said, helping her up. "We'll talk to Dad. He knows people all over the city. I'm sure he'll be able to help."

Chapter 21

"Mrs Coleman?" the baker said thoughtfully. "And she and her hubby run an inn, do they, something with 'bell' in the name? Is that all you can remember?"

Megan nodded. "Can you think of anywhere, Mr Bradley? I've tried all the streets around here for as far as I can walk." She finished her bowl of stew and drew a deep breath of satisfaction. "That's the best dinner I've had for – oh, I don't know how long."

"There's some more if you want it," Mrs Bradley said, and Megan looked at the pot longingly and then shook her head.

"I don't remember ever being offered food I couldn't eat! I don't think I've ever been so full before."

The baker was still thinking about Megan's grandmother. "I don't know anywhere with 'bell' in the name apart from Aggie's place. And I've had a look through the local street directory. There's a few Colemans, but no one with the initial A. I reckon there's some mistake in the address. Have you got the paper with you?"

Megan sighed. "It was in my purse when it was stolen. I've tried and tried to remember it, but I can't. The last time I looked at it was when I showed it to

Sally, a girl I met when I first came to London. We earned some money singing together and then she showed me which bus to get on to come here."

"You showed it to her?" Tom said eagerly. "Well, perhaps she'll remember. Where does she live?"

But Megan could only look at him helplessly and say it was somewhere near Paddington Station. "I walked quite a long way. I don't know what the streets were called."

Mr Bradley gave her an exasperated look, but Tom shrugged and said, "She's not used to big cities, Dad. She's always lived in a small village and known every street. Isn't that right, Meg?"

She nodded, grateful for his understanding. "We only had one long street, really, and a few alleyways. I always knew where everybody lived. I didn't even know that streets had names, like they do here."

"But there must be some way we could find this girl," Tom went on. "Where did you sing? In taverns?"

"Yes." She was ashamed to say that she couldn't remember their names either, and cudgelled her brains. "I think I might be able to find it again though, if we went to where I got on the omnibus."

"That's the ticket!" Tom gazed excitedly at his father. "If we go to Paddington Station and walk from there – and find out where you catch the bus to Kensington—"

"But there's buses all over the place coming to Kensington," his father objected. "And if the young lady was only there once, and hardly knew where she was—"

"It's the only chance we've got." Tom looked at Megan. "What do you say?"

She nodded. The idea of finding Sally again gave her new hope. If Sally could only remember the name of her grandmother's inn… But then the light died from her eyes.

"How can I go, with my foot like this? I can't even walk across the room, let alone tramp the streets."

"I'll go," Tom declared. "After all, it can't be too hard to find a girl called Sally who sings in public houses. Especially one who sang with a Welsh girl once." He grinned at her. "You ought to do that here. Tell old Aggie you'll sing for your supper instead of washing dishes. People like a bit of a song."

"They do when they've got money to spend," the baker said. "Nobody's got any to spare now. Look what happened tonight. And it's going to get worse, mark my words. Why, it's not even Christmas yet. If this is what it's like now, what's it going to be like in January?"

January. The very name had a chilly sound. Megan thought of the winter, grinding on across the country, bringing work to a standstill everywhere. Bringing poverty, disease and starvation over the whole of England and Wales.

Wales. She thought of her mother and brothers struggling to earn enough money to keep themselves and the little ones fed. And Morgan Jones, sitting in her father's armchair like a great spider in its web, grabbing up everything that came within reach.

I've got to find Grandma, she thought. I've got to.

Chapter 22

Aggie was not at all pleased when Tom took Megan back and told her about the accident on the ice.

"So you expect me ter keep you in luxury while yer foot gets better," she raged. "Think you can lay about like Lady Muck while the rest of us does all the work – and you not bin 'ere five minutes. Well, you can think again, that's what. If the baker's boy got yer into this trouble, the baker's boy can get yer out. There ain't no room fer fairy queens round 'ere!"

"It wasn't Tom's fault," Megan protested, but Aggie had turned away to serve a pot of ale. When the customer had moved away, she turned back.

"If you 'adn't gone to the ice fair, it wouldn't never 'ave 'appened," she said unarguably. "What use are yer goin' ter be ter me now, eh? Tell me that."

"I could sit on a stool and peel vegetables," Megan began, but Tom interrupted her.

"She could sing. Megan's got a beautiful voice. She sang in Paddington before she came here."

"Paddington?" Aggie said suspiciously. "I thought she come from Wales."

"I did. But the first night I was in London, I met a

girl who was singing in the public houses and we sang together. We earned quite a lot of money."

"I ain't payin' yer nothin'," Aggie said at once, but Megan shook her head.

"I wouldn't ask for money. Just so long as you let me stay here till I can work properly again."

Aggie thought for a minute or two, chewing her lip. Then she said, "What good's it goin' ter do, you singin'? People don't 'ave no money to pay fer that these days."

"It would bring the customers in," Tom said. "Even if they only buy one drink, it's better they should buy it here than down in the Frog and Nightgown, isn't it? And a full house brings in even more – they think the beer must be good!"

"There's nothin' wrong with my beer," Aggie said automatically. She looked at Megan. "I'd want yer to do yer work too, mind. You needn't think a bit o' caterwaulin's goin' ter be enough ter keep yer."

Megan nodded. She would have agreed to anything, just to keep a roof over her head. "I can peel vegetables. And help Betsy."

Aggie sniffed. At last she said, grudgingly, "Well, all right then. You can stop 'ere an' we'll see 'ow you manage. So long as you earns yer keep, I s'pose it's better than 'avin' ter look fer someone else."

She went to serve another customer and Tom looked ruefully at Megan. "I've a feeling you're going to find yourself working even harder!"

"I don't care," Megan said stoutly. "So long as I

don't have to go and live on the streets." She thought of the gaunt, frozen faces of the people huddled in doorways, and shuddered.

Tom said, "Look, Meggie, I'm sure you could come and live with us if it got too bad. Ma wouldn't let you starve or freeze, nor would Dad. They'd find you a corner somewhere."

Megan smiled but shook her head. "I'd rather make my own way. And I don't want to leave Etty – she needs someone to look after her. As long as I can stay here, I'll be all right."

Tom looked around at the shabby taproom with its stained, peeling walls and ceiling, dark brown with smoke, festooned with cobwebs. The kitchen was even worse, every surface greasy, the table grimy from the piles of dirty vegetables that were dumped there every day. Betsy cleaned off a bit now and then for rolling pastry, but apart from that it was rarely touched. His father would have had a fit if the bakery was in that state.

"I don't like you being here," he said. "It's no place for a girl like you."

Megan smiled and touched his hand. "Where d'you think I come from, Tom? Buckingham Palace, is it? We're as poor as church mice in the valleys, and if we scrubbed the whole place out three times a day it still wouldn't be any cleaner. At least everything's not covered in coal dust here!"

After Tom had gone, she hobbled into the kitchen where Betsy had already put a high stool at the table for her to sit on. The taproom was full of the evening's customers but she was too weary to sing tonight. Instead, she sat at the table and began to scrape the carrots for yet another stew.

"Gawd knows 'ow many more of those there'll be," Betsy said gloomily. "It's so cold now they can't get 'em out of the ground. Nor parsnips, nor swede. Once they've used up the clamps, that'll be the lot till it thaws out again."

Megan sighed. Everything was in short supply now, and what there was had shot up in price. She made sure she was scraping the carrots as thinly as possible. Nothing must be wasted.

Clarrie came into the kitchen and gave Megan an unfriendly look.

"So you're back," she said, as if Megan had been gone for days instead of just the afternoon. "I 'spose you think we're all goin' ter run round after yer, just because you give yer ankle a bit of a twist! Well, you won't get no sympathy from me – you shouldn't never've gone. I told you to keep clear of Tom Bradley."

"It wasn't Tom's fault," Megan said, and Clarrie snorted.

"Who said it was? Serves yer right, that's what I say. Goin' off gallivantin' and leavin' the rest of us ter do the work. An' now you reckon yer goin' ter sing. Sing! That ain't work."

Megan said nothing. Whatever she said, it would be wrong for Clarrie. She went on scraping carrots and after a moment or two Clarrie snorted again and went back to the taproom.

"She's jealous," Etty remarked, coming in from the scullery with a pile of washed dishes. "She wishes it was her had gone to the ice fair with Tom."

Megan spent the rest of the evening sitting on the stool, preparing vegetables. Even when Betsy had stopped making stew for the night, there were still plenty to be done for the next day, and Megan's eyes were burning and red from peeling and chopping onions before Aggie decided that it was time to close. She eased herself down from the high stool and leant on the table, her ankle throbbing.

"You ought to put it up," Etty said. "Here, lean on me or you'll never get up the stairs."

Etty was so frail that Megan felt she would break into pieces if she leant her weight on her. She smiled and shook her head. "I'll manage."

But she was grateful, all the same, for Etty's help in getting her shoes and stockings off. Her foot was still badly swollen and the bruises were even darker than when Tom had looked at them, but the cold poultice Mrs Bradley had put on did seem to have helped, and Etty offered to run down and get some more ice for a fresh one.

"Lucky, really, that it's so bitter cold," she said cheerfully, returning with a long icicle she had broken off a low roof. "I'll smash this up an' wrap it round your ankle with this bit of rag. Let's 'ope it doesn't melt too quick – you'll 'ave a wet bed!"

Megan shivered. The ice didn't seem likely to melt very quickly up here in this attic. She flinched as Etty bound up her ankle again, but soon it began to throb with warmth. It was queer how a cold poultice did that, but it worked.

She lay down on the hard, lumpy mattress, thinking of the day she had just spent. So much had happened – the ice fair, seeing Grandma, the fall on the ice. The drive home in a hansom cab (something she had never dreamed she would do), the terrible sight of the gaunt, famished crowds trudging hopelessly through the streets, crying out for bread to fill their craving bellies. The terror of the riot and the dreadful moments when she had believed Tom to be injured – or even killed – under the trampling hooves of the police horses.

And then the warmth and kindness of the Bradleys. The easy comfort of their kitchen, filled with the rich smell of newly-baked bread. The look in Tom's eyes as he'd smiled at her across the big, scrubbed table, and his gentleness as he'd brought her back to the inn.

"*I don't like seeing you here,*" he'd said. "*It's no place for a girl like you.*"

A girl like you. Nobody had said anything like that to her before.

She fell asleep with a smile on her lips, no longer noticing the pain of her ankle.

Chapter 23

By Christmas, Megan's ankle was almost better. She could stand and walk well, though it sometimes gave way under her – especially if she stepped on an uneven paving stone – giving her an agonizing twinge of pain. And she was nervous of walking on ice in case she slipped again.

She had now established herself as a firm favourite in the alehouse with her singing, and the taproom was filled night after night with customers. She had learnt some of the latest music-hall songs and she sang these with a verve which had the drinkers clapping and cheering. But it was her Welsh melodies, sung with a piercing sweetness which brought tears to even the most hardened eye, that made her different from the other alehouse singers. It didn't matter that the words couldn't be understood. The sadness of Megan's throbbing tones told clearly enough what the song was saying, and the emotions were reflected in every face.

"She gets right into yer 'eart," a big, burly Cockney said as he paid for a huge tankard of ale. "I dunno what it is, but when I 'ears that voice of 'ers singin' like a bird – better'n a bird – well, it sorta makes me think of things I ain't never 'ad. Like as if there must be something better round the corner, if only you knew 'ow ter find it."

"It's a big corner, then," his mate observed, stamping down a few strands of tobacco in his pipe. "I ain't never found the way round it."

While Megan had been unable to go out, Tom had been to Paddington several times to look for Sally. He had followed the route of the omnibus, starting at Paddington Station and walking up and down every street, asking in the alehouses whether anyone knew a girl called Sally who sang there. The innkeepers shook their heads and the girls who worked there stared at him with suspicion.

"Whatcher want 'er for?" one of them asked him. "Pinch summat off yer, did she?"

Tom shook his head. "I want to find her for a friend."

"Won't I do?" asked another girl, sidling up to him. She had black curls and sooty eyes, but her blouse was dirty and the collar torn. "I bet I can sing as good as this Sally."

Tom looked at her with distaste and shook his head. He went outside and stared up and down the street, wondering where to try next.

The next time, he turned in a different direction and walked right up the Edgware Road and halfway along Maida Vale before giving up. Looking for Sally, he thought, was worse than looking for Megan's grandmother.

"The trouble is, I don't know what either of them looks like," he told Megan. "I might walk past them a dozen times and never know."

Megan sighed. She had still heard nothing from her family, although she'd written twice to tell them where she was.

"I'm wondering if I ought to stay in London," she confessed. "I'm not doing any good here, and they need my earnings. But suppose I went back and Morgan Jones threw me out. That wouldn't help anyone." She sighed. "If Aggie would give me money I could send it to them, but she won't give me a penny, says I'm still not earning it."

"That's rubbish," Tom said angrily. "There's nobody here works harder than you do." He took Megan's hand. "Meggie, why don't you come and live with us? There's room and Ma says she'd welcome your help – but she wouldn't make a slave of you like Aggie does. She looks on you like a daughter now, you know."

Megan blushed. Since the night of the riot, she had been to the bakehouse several times and felt more at home there every time she walked through the door. She was treated more as a member of the family than a visitor, and often helped prepare the supper or wash the dishes – chores which Tom's mother tried to prevent her doing. "You do enough of that at Aggie Crowther's place," she said.

"Ah, but it's different here, see," Megan had answered. "It's a pleasure here – and besides, I have some of the supper myself, don't I!"

127

Aggie was as mean as ever with the food she allowed her servants. It wasn't so bad for Megan, who was given a good meal at the bakehouse once or twice a week, nor for Betsy the cook, who could sneak a few titbits into her mouth. Even Clarrie and Ruth could steal a morsel or two off a customer's plate as they carried them through the taproom. But little Etty, who needed good food more than any of them, had no such chances. Slaving away at the sink, few stray morsels came her way, and she was growing thinner and paler every day. Worse still, her cough was beginning to frighten Megan. It kept her awake at night, racking the frail little body as if it would tear her to pieces, and she would lie shuddering with cold under the thin blanket they shared, while her body burned as if it were on fire.

"I can't leave Etty and come to live with you," Megan said to Tom when he asked her again to move to the bakehouse. "I'm afraid of what might happen to her. And she's been a good friend to me."

Tom sighed. He knew that Etty was really ill and would probably not survive much longer. He couldn't ask Megan to abandon her friend. But the city was in the grip of the worst winter that anyone could remember. People were dying every day, from cold, from starvation, from sheer weakness and despair.

And with every day that passed, with every bitter wind that blew, the chances of finding Megan's grandmother seemed to grow slimmer.

Chapter 24

"You really come from Wales?" one of the customers asked her a night or two later. "Or did someone learn yer them songs?"

"No, I'm really Welsh," Megan said, conscious of the lilt in her voice. "Can't you tell?"

He looked at her. He was a stranger, who had never been into the alehouse before. He looked different from most of the other customers – not quite so rough. He wore a neckerchief that was almost clean and he looked as though he shaved at least twice a week.

"There's another girl what sings Welsh songs," he said. "Leastways, I've 'eard 'er sing one. She don't sing 'em as good as you, though. I don't reckon she's Welsh."

Megan, who had been about to start another song, stared at him. Her mouth was open, ready to begin. She closed it slowly and then opened it again to ask, with sudden excitement, "What girl? Where did you hear her?"

"Lambeth way," he said. "There's a place called the Elephant and Castle – everyone knows it. She was 'angin' around there."

"The Elephant and Castle? Lambeth?" Megan felt

the disappointment trickle over her skin. "Oh. I – I thought she might be someone I knew."

"Well, maybe she is," the man said. "She 'adn't been there long, I know that. I'm a reg'lar there, see – I knows 'em all."

A sudden screech from Aggie made Megan jump and she hastily began to sing again. But with her eyes on the man's face, she began to sing the little ballad she had taught Sally, and was rewarded by the recognition on his face. It must be Sally he's heard, she thought. It can't be a coincidence. As soon as I get a chance, I'll ask him.

But there wasn't a chance. By the time she'd finished the song, he had paid for his drink and left. She saw his back disappear through the door as she sang the last notes, and felt the hot tears of frustration brim in her eyes.

"Cor, that was lovely," said a woman nearby. "You could tell it was a sad song by the way yer eyes all filled up. I do like a sad song."

"I don't," her companion said shortly. "I likes a bit of cheerfulness. Give us summat to brighten us up a bit, can't yer, gal? We got enough misery to put up with these days."

Megan stared hopelessly at him. Cheerfulness? When her only hope of finding Sally had just walked out into the dark street? But Aggie was glaring at her across the room and she knew she must give the customers what they wanted, or she would be pushed out in the street too, to starve or freeze.

The Elephant and Castle. He must have been joking – there couldn't possibly be a place with such an outlandish name as that. And what was the other name he'd used? Lambeth? Somehow that didn't sound any more likely.

Tom would know. She would ask him at the first possible moment.

"Of course there's a place called the Elephant and Castle," Tom said. "Haven't you ever heard of it? It's famous."

"Why? Why is it famous? Anyway, it can't be that famous – we've never heard of it in Wales," Megan said, feeling rather nettled. But Tom only laughed.

"You've never heard of anything, in Wales! Ah, don't look like that, Meggie – I was only teasing. Anyway, the Elephant and Castle is a public house, like Aggie's. As for why it's famous, I suppose it's just because it's such a strange name. But they've got a sign which shows you what it means – an Indian elephant, with a howdah on its back. That's a sort of little wooden turret for a rajah to ride in," he explained hastily, seeing Megan's blank look.

Megan didn't know what a rajah was either, but she was determined not to say so. Tom was never unkind, but he was often surprised at the things which he knew and she didn't. He'd told her not to worry about it – "You know all sorts of things I don't know, about mining and the Welsh mountains and things like that," he'd said – but she still felt ignorant compared with him.

"D'you know where this elephant place is, then?" she asked. "Have you ever been there?"

Tom shook his head. "I don't know London south of the river. But it'd be easy enough to find. The only thing is — well, Meggie, how likely d'you think it is that this is Sally? You don't know she ever went there. There might be a hundred girls singing Welsh songs."

"It's a chance. It's the first chance I've had."

"I know, but—"

"Won't you go?" Megan asked, staring at him. "Is that what you're saying? You're tired of it, aren't you — tired of traipsing all over London looking for a girl you don't even know. Why don't you just say so? Why don't you?"

"I'm not tired of it," Tom said. "I just don't want to see you disappointed again. And besides—" He stopped, looking uncomfortable.

"Besides what?"

"I can't go and look this week. I've got to do Joe's deliveries as well as mine. And we're making twice as much bread for the workhouse; they're giving out as much as they can. I won't have time to do anything more until this cold weather's over."

"But by then Sally might have gone somewhere else—"

"I can't help it," Tom said miserably. "I've got work to do."

"And I've got to find my grandmother—"

"There are people *starving* out there," Tom said suddenly, losing his temper. "Don't they matter? You saw those rioters. There've been more riots like that, you know there have. People getting hurt, killed. People dying of hunger. And all you can think about is finding your grandmother. She'll still be there when all this is over, Megan. You can find her then."

"*She* might still be there," Megan said bitterly, "but what about my poor Mam in Wales, and my brothers and the little ones? *They* could be dying of hunger too. But you don't know them. They're nothing to you. You don't care about them – why should you?"

She turned and marched out of the kitchen. Tom caught her in the scullery, where she was bending over the low sink and scrubbing frantically at a pan that Betsy had burned that morning. He stood unhappily behind her, waiting for her to turn round, but she kept her back to him.

"Meggie. Meggie, don't say things like that. Of course I care about them. But I can't just walk out and leave my father to manage on his own. I've got to think of him too."

"Of course you have," Megan said in a tight, unhappy voice. "I know you have. It's all right, Tom. Don't you worry about me. You go back now and help your da; he needs you." She looked up at him briefly, her eyes shining with tears. "I'll manage fine."

"Megan, I *want* to help you—" he began, but Megan walked past him and straight through the kitchen to the taproom. He heard her voice as she began to sing, and stood undecided for a few moments. Then Clarrie came through and gave him a sharp glance.

"It's no good you 'angin' about 'ere. She's given yer the elbow, can't yer see it?" She came a little nearer and gave him a sly look. "Don't you bother yerself with 'er any more, Tom. Remember me – we've always bin pals, ain't we?"

Tom stared at her for a moment. Then, without saying a word, he picked up the big, empty bread basket and swung out of the kitchen, letting a cold blast of air whistle through before the door slammed shut behind him.

Clarrie shrugged and picked up two more bowls of stew. Because of the continuing bitter weather, both meat and vegetables were almost impossible to come by now, and it was more like workhouse gruel. Goodness knew what the inmates were getting in the workhouses!

"Please yerself, Tom Bradley," she said. "There's plenty more fish in the sea. I'm sure *I* ain't bothered."

Chapter 25

Aggie was reluctant to let Megan have any time off, but since there were not many customers during the first few days of January, and Megan hadn't had an afternoon out since her accident on the ice, she gave way eventually, and begrudgingly allowed her a couple of hours. Megan slipped out immediately, before her employer could change her mind.

"You will be careful, won't you?" Etty begged. "I wouldn't know what to do if anything 'appened to you."

"Nothing's going to happen to me, *bach*," Megan said comfortingly. "And I'll be back before you know it. Just don't let the old faggot make you work too hard. The vegetables are all ready, look."

She had been doing a lot of Etty's work for her lately, hoping that Aggie hadn't noticed. If there was any suspicion that Etty wasn't able to pull her weight, it would be the workhouse for her – Aggie had already threatened her with that. Etty was terrified that she would carry out her threat.

"I'd rather die than go there," she said. "And I *would* die, too – I'd be dead in a week. She might as well let me die here."

"Nah. Bad for trade," Betsy said, shaking her head. "Customers don't like it if there's corpses all over the place. Not unless they're meant for a pie, that is!" She laughed harshly.

"Well, I don't think they'd find much meat on you, Etty, so there's not much point in dying anywhere," Megan said, trying to lighten the atmosphere. "Anyway, you're not to do any such thing before I come back, see? Never mind 'you can't manage without me' – *I* can't manage without *you*."

Etty laughed and waved her off more cheerfully. Megan set off up the street.

It was still bitterly cold. The temperature was below freezing and had been for weeks now – sometimes it seemed as if it had been for ever. She shivered and pulled her shawl more closely around her body, wrapping the ends about her hands. Once, when she was very little, Grandma had knitted her a pair of mittens, and she had never forgotten their warmth.

The thought of Grandma brought tears to her eyes again and she scolded herself. Crying wasn't going to help anyone! But she couldn't help the sharp ache in her throat, the feeling of fullness pulsing behind her eyes. It'll be all right when I find Grandma, she thought. And surely Sally will remember the address. We'll be able to go straight there.

She had no money for an omnibus, and in any case there were hardly any around on the icy streets. Too many horses had slipped and broken their legs, and now not many cabs or wagons would venture out. Besides, most people were keeping what little money they had for food and fuel. There was none for luxuries.

Because she had searched so hard already, Megan knew the streets of Kensington well. She had asked Betsy the way to Lambeth and now she made her way to Hyde Park, where there were still entertainments and refreshment tents on the frozen Serpentine, though only the rich had the money to spend on them now and they were crowded with beggars. She stood for a few minutes gazing at the scene and re-membering the day Tom had taken her there.

Her fingers felt something hard in the pocket of her skirt and she drew it out. It was the tiny wooden doll Tom had given her at the fair that day. She gazed at it and felt a lump come into her throat.

I wish I hadn't quarrelled with him, she thought sadly. He's been a good friend, and of course he's got to help his father. And he looked so unhappy when I walked out of the kitchen...

But there was nothing to be done about it now and, determined to make it up with him the minute she got back, Megan turned away from the Serpentine and walked on across Hyde Park. At the far corner, remembering Betsy's instructions, she crossed the wide road to walk down Constitution Hill and came to the gates of Buckingham Palace.

Once again, she could not help stopping. There was a small crowd standing by the tall, wrought-iron gates, and inside she could see the red-jacketed figures of the Guards marching up and down. Their high black busbies made them look at least seven feet tall, and underneath the furry hats their faces were stern. They looked ready to defend their Queen against all dangers.

"What's happening?" she asked a young woman beside her. The girl turned and smiled.

"They're changing the Guard. Those ones have just finished their duty and they're handing over to the others. There's always a ceremony about it – they can't just say well, it's your turn now. It's lovely to watch."

Megan watched, fascinated, as the soldiers marched up and down inside the fence, then turned as she heard a gasp from the crowd. The great gates were opening and a large black carriage was approaching. Inside she could see a small round face peering out, with a bearded one close beside it. There were other faces too – two or three children and a bright-eyed young man.

"It's the *Queen*," the young woman whispered in awe. "And Prince Albert, and some of the children. Oh, what luck!"

The crowd were clapping and cheering, and the men had taken off their hats. The carriage was almost at the gates now, so close to Megan that she could almost have reached out and touched it. Trembling with awe and delight, she gazed up at the windows.

The woman inside looked no older than her own mother, and far less careworn. Her skin was smooth, her hair shining beneath the little cap she wore. She glanced out as the horses slowed to draw the carriage through the gateway, and her eyes met Megan's.

It seemed to be for an eternity that they stared at each other. And then Megan, hardly knowing what she did, dropped a deep curtsy. And the Queen smiled.

The carriage was gone, the gates swung closed. The Guards had completed their ceremony and the crowd began to drift away. Megan stood, still dazed, her arms wrapping her shawl tightly around her body.

I've seen the Queen, she thought. I've seen Queen Victoria. And she's seen *me*!

Surely that must be an omen. Surely it must mean that everything would be all right.

With a little skip of joy, she hurried on her way.

Chapter 26

The easiest route, Betsy had told her, was to go down Birdcage Walk alongside St James's Park, then along Great George Street to Westminster Bridge and follow the main road to Lambeth. Anyone would tell her the way to the Elephant and Castle.

I must be the only person in London who doesn't know where it it, Megan thought as she trudged through the icy streets. She gazed about her, awed by the magnificent buildings. Their names were a mystery – the Institution of Civil Engineers, the Surveyors' Institute, Eyers' Bank – what did it all mean? What went on in those huge places? What did people do in there?

Most imposing of all were the Houses of Parliament. At first sight, Megan thought it must be another palace, and when she asked a woman passing by, she was told that yes, it was a palace – the Palace of Westminster. "But the Queen don't live there. It's all the Government, see. Mr Palmerston, and Disraeli and Gladstone, all that lot. That's where they decides what's goin' ter 'appen to us."

Megan nodded and looked again at the enormous

building with its tall new clock tower. She had heard of Mr Palmerston. He was Prime Minister – that meant he was in charge. She was vague about the others the woman had mentioned, but she was tired of showing her ignorance so she smiled her thanks and walked on, feeling almost dizzy.

Who would have thought that little Megan Price, from the valleys of the Rhondda, would ever come to London and see such sights?

The Houses of Parliament stood on the banks of the River Thames. "You'll 'ave ter cross there," Betsy had told her. "Westminster Bridge, that is. Don't fall in, mind!"

It wouldn't be too easy to fall in, Megan thought, looking over the railings, but it would be a horrible thing to do. The river flowed below, a grey-brown, murky sludge thick with rubbish and slime. There were boats moving on it too, adding to the debris as their crews slung buckets of waste over the side. It looked as if all London used the Thames as a drain, and the stink made her feel sick.

By the time she reached the south bank, her legs were aching and her nose and ears were raw from the bitter wind. But she had no time to rest. Aggie would be waiting for her to come back for the evening's custom, and there was barely time to do what she had to do before turning back.

Thankful for the warm shawl Tom's mother had given her at Christmas, Megan hurried on. The streets were poorer now, away from the grand buildings of

Westminster, and she was surrounded by decaying tenements, houses that had once been the mansions of the wealthy but had been left to rot.

There was a strange, almost frightening silence in the streets. A few children, scantily clothed even in this freezing weather, scuffled in the gutters and beggars huddled against the slimy walls like bundles of old rags, stretching out claw-like hands in imploring appeal. But for the most part, people shuffled along the icy pavements without speaking, avoiding each other's eyes, as if each one was sunk in private despair.

Tom's right, Megan thought. People are starving everywhere. I'm lucky to have a roof over my head and enough food to keep me alive.

At the corner of the road, she hesitated. Ask someone, Betsy had told her. But there wasn't anyone Megan dared ask. An old man shambled along the pavement towards her, mumbling and dribbling into a matted grey beard. An old woman was sitting on a broken wall, singing in a raucous voice and breaking off to swear at passers-by. And there were a few youths lounging in a doorway, watching her.

Megan quickened her steps again. She could have asked them, but she was afraid of the expression in their eyes.

She passed a long, yellowy-grey wall which loomed ominously above the road. Behind it was a large building, with rows of small barred windows in its sides. It looked as grim as a prison, but when Megan came to the big gateway she saw its name carved into the stone above the arch: *Bethlehem Lunatic Hospital.*

Megan shuddered. All the pleasure of seeing Buckingham Palace and the Queen and her consort had evaporated. She wondered if Queen Victoria had ever been here, or even knew that such a place existed. She wondered what it was like for those poor sufferers inside.

"Whatcher gawpin' at?" The rasping voice jerked her out of her thoughts and she realized that she had stopped and was staring in through the big gateway. "Wanter come in, do yer?"

Megan stared at the speaker. It was one of the guards who stood at the gate, a big, coarse-faced man who carried a long pike. He made a move towards her and she backed away and fled, hearing his sneering guffaw behind her. It was several minutes before she dared to stop.

Now she was truly lost. She pressed her hand to her side, breathing hard as she stared about her. A street nameplate caught her eye and she went forwards uncertainly.

"What's the matter, duck?" The new voice had the roughness of the Cockney accent, but there was a touch of warmth in it too, a hint of kindness. "You look as if you're lost."

Megan paused, looking at the woman. She was poorly dressed, but there was a decency about her, as if she tried to keep herself clean and tidy. Her shawl had been torn but it had been mended, and the frill of her bonnet was white. Her face looked clean too, with hardly any dirt ingrained into the hundred tiny creases which her cheeks folded into when she smiled, as if they'd been used to smiling like that for a very long time.

"I am," Megan confessed. "I'm looking for the Elephant and Castle, but I think I've come the wrong way."

The woman looked surprised and then interested as Megan spoke. "The Elephant and Castle? Oh, you're not too far out of the way. Just go along here beside Lambeth Infirmary –" she indicated another long, grim wall running beside the road – "to the corner where the workhouse gate is, and then turn left up Hale Street out into St George's Road. Go right along there and along New Kent Road and you'll see the Elephant. You can't miss it." She paused for a moment. "Are you all right, love? It's not the sort of place for a young girl to be going all on her own, if she's a stranger."

"I'm quite all right, thank you very much," Megan said quickly, anxious to be on her way. "I'm really grateful, but I must hurry – I have to be back at work you see –" She was already moving away as she spoke and for a moment she thought the woman was about to put out her hand to delay her. But then she seemed to change her mind.

"Well, you know your own business best, I'm sure. But why don't you let me walk along with you? It don't make any difference to me to go that way, and I don't like to think of a respectable young girl like you wandering these streets, specially with it getting dark."

Megan glanced about her. She hadn't realized evening was approaching already, but it was still the darkest part of winter and a mass of clouds, brown and yellow as bruises, hung over the roofs. The air felt cold and dry, as if it might snow.

"Thank you," she said, realizing how easy it would be to get lost again. "Thank you very much; it's kind of you."

The woman fell in beside her and they walked swiftly together through the streets. Megan was silent, her thoughts busy, her heart thumping quickly with excitement.

In a few minutes she could be talking to Sally, and if Sally could only remember the name of her grandmother's inn, she might, this very evening, find her grandmother as well.

Chapter 27

It was further than she had expected to the Elephant and Castle. Her companion led her through a maze of tiny alleyways, explaining that it was quicker this way, but too complicated to have directed her there. Megan scurried beside her, almost too tired now to keep up with the woman's brisk stride. She wondered how she was going to walk back. But perhaps she wouldn't have to, if she found Grandma tonight.

But I'll have to go back and fetch Etty, she thought. I can't leave her there by herself. And I'll have to make it up with Tom. But all that would be sorted out easily, once she was with Grandma. Grandma would see to everything.

"Here, I've just remembered," the woman said, stopping so suddenly that Megan nearly walked into her. "The Elephant don't open till six. It won't be any good going there yet." She looked at Megan in dismay, then her face cleared. "Look, why don't you come and have a cuppa with me? It'll pass the time and you look as if you could do with a bit of a warm. I live just round the corner."

"Oh, I couldn't…" Megan began, feeling suddenly

anxious. Suppose something were to happen to her. Nobody knew where she was, nobody would come to search. But the woman smiled, and she felt ashamed of her suspicions.

"Course you could. What's to stop you? It won't take ten minutes to get the fire going and put on the kettle. I can't leave you out here in the cold."

"It's very kind of you," Megan said gratefully, following her new friend down a dark little alley. "But if I could just sit inside for a while – you don't have to give me tea—"

"Don't be silly, duck. A cuppa tea won't break me. I ain't like some of them that lives round here, you know, not got two pennies to rub together. I'm careful, I save my money, always have, so I don't have to go short. Always put a bit by for a rainy day, that's what my old mum used to tell me, and that's what I've always done. Here we are."

She stopped and pushed open a door. Megan followed her into a narrow passage which was plunged into pitch darkness as the door closed. For a moment, she felt oddly frightened. What was she doing here, in this strange house with a woman she didn't know? But then she shook herself and scolded away her sudden panic. There was nothing to be afraid of. The woman was simply being kind. You only had to look at her to know that she wouldn't harm anyone.

"Sit down there, love," the woman said, bustling about. She lit a candle and Megan saw a small room with a range at one end, the coals faintly glowing.

Two rather battered but clean armchairs stood before it, one occupied by a large tabby cat. There was a table and three or four chairs, and on the walls she could see some pictures. They were rather dim but they looked like religious paintings, with tall, robed figures and camels, or clusters of angels with shimmering wings.

But what struck her most about the room was its warmth. After hours out in the freezing streets, Megan had almost forgotten what it was like to be warm. She moved forwards, her hands held out towards the glowing coals.

"There you are. It don't take a minute to get the fire burning up." The woman set an old black kettle on the hob and turned to look down at Megan, who had taken the chair not occupied by the cat. "Well, you're a pretty little thing, aren't you! What's your name?"

"Megan Price," Megan said shyly.

"Megan Price! That's not a London name. Where are you from?"

"Wales. I came to find my grandmother."

"Came to find your granny. Fancy that. And d'you know where your granny lives?"

Megan shook her head. "She runs an inn somewhere in London. She gave me her address but I've lost it."

"Lost it!" said the woman, who seemed to need to repeat everything in order to understand it. "Well, so what are you doing round these parts? Is this where you think she'll be?"

Megan shook her head. "I think she's in Kensington. But I've looked everywhere there. I'm hoping to find a girl I met when I first came to London – I told her about my grandmother, see, and I'm hoping she'll remember the address. But I don't really know where she is, either."

"You don't know where *she* is? Well, you are in a pickle, aren't you? And I daresay you've not had time to make any other friends in London, have you?"

"Well…" Megan began, thinking of Tom. Was he still her friend? And there was Etty. She certainly couldn't count Clarrie or Ruth as friends, nor Aggie. But before she could say any more, the kettle began to sing and the woman snatched it from the hob and flung in a handful of dusty-looking tea. She found a couple of chipped earthenware cups and poured a stream of dark liquid into them.

"Ain't got no milk," she said tersely, handing Megan one of the cups, "but you can have some sugar if you want."

Megan shook her head. They'd never been able to afford sugar in the valleys. The woman took two heaped teaspoonfuls and stirred it in.

"My name's Peg," she announced suddenly. "They all know me round these parts. I run a hotel here."

"A hotel?" Megan barely understood the meaning of the word. "Is that a sort of inn?"

"Sort of," Peg agreed. "I let out rooms. But I only let to respectable young ladies – young ladies like yourself. I'm very particular. I don't take in just anybody.

And I like to look on my young ladies as daughters –
I like to be a family."

Megan said nothing. The idea of being in a family
filled her with yearning. She thought of Mam and
Owen and the little ones. How were they getting on?
How were they managing without her?

I never meant to be away this long, she thought,
staring into the flames. I thought I'd come and find
Grandma and she'd come straight back and make
everything all right again. I didn't have any idea what
it was really going to be like.

"So if you want to take the chance, you'd be
welcome," Peg was saying, and Megan jumped
guiltily. She hadn't heard a word.

"What d'you say? I'm sorry – I didn't hear – it's so
warm and comfortable in here…" Megan stammered,
and Peg laughed.

"That's all right, duck. You drink your tea. You'll
feel better with something hot inside you." She
watched indulgently as Megan sipped the strong
liquid. It flowed down inside her, making a hot path
all the way down her chest and into her stomach.
"What I was saying was, why don't you move in here
– just till you find your gran, that is. And I daresay I'd
be able to help there, too. I know most people round
these parts. You'd have plenty of company, and a
warm fire to sit by and enough to eat and drink – I
treat my girls well, I do. What d'you say?" she asked
again.

"Move in here? But – I can't. I haven't got any

money. My purse was stolen. That's how I lost Grandma's address. And—"

She had been going to say that she must go back to Aggie's, that she couldn't leave Etty, but Peg broke in before she could form the words.

"Who said anything about money? I didn't say you had to pay, did I? Look, I can see you're down on your luck. I'm offering you a helping hand, that's all. A bit of Christian charity." She leaned forwards and put her hand over Megan's. "I'll tell you the truth, gal. You'd be doing me a favour. See, you put me in mind of someone else. Well –" she touched the corner of her eye with the hem of her skirt – "matter of fact, she was my own gal. My daughter. She'd have bin about your age now – and you've got a look of her, somehow. Same colour eyes, same hair. Same way of looking when you ain't sure of yourself. I like looking at you, that's the plain and simple truth of it. I'd like to have you round the place – even if it's only for a few days."

Megan stared at her. "What – what happened to your daughter?" she asked softly.

Peg looked into the fire. "What always happens? She took ill – died. Three years ago, it was, and I've not got over it yet. Never will. But I've set out since then to help young girls like my Rosie. That's why I'd like to help you."

I ought to go back, Megan thought. I can't leave Etty. And I must make it up with Tom. But…

She glanced around the room. It was plain and

shabby, but it was warm. There were chairs and a table and pictures on the walls. It was a home.

She thought of going out into the streets again, searching for Grandma, searching for Sally, and then facing the long trudge back to Aggie's. Perhaps being turned out when she got there, for being away so long.

She thought of the bitter cold, of the people huddled in doorways, the skeletal hands stretched out, begging for alms.

"I've got a friend, where I've been staying," she said hesitantly. "She – she isn't very strong but she does as much as she can. She'd help cook meals and things like that if she could come here too. Could I – could I bring her along?"

Peg's face broke into its mass of tiny, smiling wrinkles. She squeezed Megan's hand and then patted it.

"Could you bring her along? Course you could! Any friend of yours is a friend of mine, and it'll do my heart good to look after the pair of you. Why, if it ain't just what my Rosie would've done herself! Always bringing home waifs and strays, she was. Kind-hearted, just like her ma. And you're the same. I can see it. I knew we'd hit it off together, knew it the minute I saw you."

She poured Megan another cup of tea. This time, she added some sugar, and tipped in some colourless liquid from a small bottle. "It's a special tonic," she said, seeing Megan's puzzled look. "It'll warm you up.

You're looking shrammed with cold, and I won't let you go out again till you've got a few roses in your cheeks. I'm going to be a mother to you, gal, a real mother."

Megan sipped. The tea tasted strange, but she supposed it was the tonic. It certainly made her feel warmer. A trail of heat spread down her chest and into her stomach, making her feel sleepy and languorous. She slipped down a little in the chair and rested her head against its back.

"That's the ticket," Peg said softly. "You just go to sleep. Have a good kip. Don't you worry about a thing. You've got old Peg now. Old Peg'll look after you."

Her voice went on, murmuring gently, blending with the singing of the kettle and the soft crackle of the fire. After a while, Megan wasn't sure which was which; a few moments later, she could hear none of them.

Peg watched a little longer. Then she spread Megan's shawl over her like a blanket. She looked down at the sleeping girl and, slowly, she smiled.

Chapter 28

It was beginning to get light when Megan woke. For a few moments she stared around the little room, grey with the chilly fingers of dawn. She looked at the pictures on the walls, at the armchair opposite the one in which she was curled, the range with its coals now dead, covered with ashes.

Where am I? she thought with sudden panic. What's happened? And then the memory rushed back. The old woman – Peg – meeting her in the street, bringing her here, talking to her so kindly. Why, she'd even offered her a home – her and Etty. And said she would help find Grandma.

Megan breathed a sigh of relief. But I shouldn't have stayed all night, she reminded herself. I meant to go back. Etty will be worried about me – and Aggie'll be furious.

Her panic returned. Suppose Peg had regretted her offer. Suppose she said she didn't want Megan here after all – and Aggie wouldn't take her back. What would she do then?

The room was very cold. She pulled her shawl closer around her, and as she did so the door opened and Peg bustled in.

"So you've woke up at last! Well, that's a good long sleep you've had and no mistake. You musta been dog-tired. I thought when I first saw you, that girl's out on her feet. Good job we ran into each other – you'd never have been able to walk all the way back to Kensington."

She set a large steaming mug and a bowl down beside Megan's chair. "There you are, my duck. Good strong tea and a bowl of porridge. That'll put heart into you. Eat it up now, and then we'll talk about what you're going to do."

Megan took the bowl gratefully. The porridge was hot and thick, and very sweet. She felt it warming her body, and while she ate it Peg busied herself with clearing out the range and relighting it. The first flames were reaching up into the chimney as Megan laid down her bowl.

"That was lovely," she said, sipping her tea. "I've never had a breakfast like that before."

"What d'you have when you're at home, then?" Peg asked.

"Oh, some bread if there is any, with a bit of dripping on it if Mam's been able to get some. And Owen takes a couple of bits down the mine. Then we have whatever there is at night – sometimes there's a bit of meat or cheese or an egg, but most often it's potatoes or a swede or something like that."

"Well, we eat a bit better than that here," Peg said. "My girls all put in a bit, you see, and we can run to a pie or a bit of stew most days. But what I won't say it's not been harder lately, what with the cold, and the markets closed a lot of the time – there just ain't the stuff about. But we get by, one way and another."

Megan wondered where the other girls were. Now that she was properly awake, she remembered hearing footsteps during the night, and voices. But nobody had come into this room and the house was quiet now. What did people do in a hotel?

"Well, you look as if you could do with a bit more kip," Peg remarked, picking up Megan's bowl and mug. "Proper worn out, you must be. You settle down again by the fire while I gets on with me work."

"Oh, no. I can't sleep now – it's morning. And I want to find Sally – and Grandma." Megan pushed the shawl aside and began to rise from the chair. "And I must go back to Kensington and let Etty know what's happening. And T—"

"You ain't going nowhere till you're looking better," Peg said, pushing her back into the chair. "I couldn't have it on me conscience. You're pale as ashes. It's a good rest you need, and warmth, and some good food inside you before you goes out there again. Why, it's cold enough to freeze the pawnbroker's brass balls off his sign!"

Megan smiled. The pawnbroker's sign of three balls, hung on a brass "monkey" above the shop doorway, was well known to be so securely fixed that almost nothing could remove it. It would have to be very cold indeed for the balls to fall off.

"I still think I ought to go—" she began, and started to get up again. But to her surprise, her legs refused to bear her. They trembled beneath her weight, and she felt her eyelids droop as a wave of sleepiness swept over her.

"You see," Peg said triumphantly. "You're not in no fit state to go wandering the streets. You stop here, my duck, till you feels better, and *then* we'll talk about going to fetch your little pal, and looking for your gran." She pressed Megan back into the chair and tucked the shawl over her again. "A good long sleep, that's what you need. And next time you wake up, there'll be a nice bowl of stew beside you." She stood beside Megan, watching until the girl's eyes were fully closed and her breathing even. "Didn't I tell you I was going to treat you as if I was your own mother?" she asked softly. "Didn't I say…?"

When Megan woke next, the light in the room seemed just the same, and for a moment or two she thought she hadn't slept at all. But as she struggled to sit up, the door opened and a small, pale face peeped around it. The two girls gazed at each other.

"Oh, you're awake," the newcomer said with relief. "I thought you weren't never goin' ter wake up. I bin lookin' in all day. I'm Lizzie."

"All *day*?" Megan echoed in astonishment. "You mean it's not morning any more?"

Lizzie came right into the room and shut the door quietly behind her. She came close to Megan and knelt beside the chair.

"You've bin asleep for hours. It's the tea. She puts something in it. It makes you sleep like the dead."

Megan stared at her. Lizzie was whispering so low

that it was difficult to know if she'd heard aright. She felt a twinge of fear. "The tonic? But she said it would make me warmer—"

"Make you sleep, you mean. An' you were still tired this morning," Lizzie said. "An' she said you could stop here. She said she'd treat you like her own daughter. I bet she even said you reminded her of her girl, Rosie, that died two or three years back."

Megan gasped. "How did you know that?"

"She says it to everyone," Lizzie said. "She said it to me when I come 'ere. She says it to all the girls. And she made us all sleep, too, so we couldn't get away."

"But why? Why should she do that?"

"So we'll stop an' work for her, of course. Look," Lizzie said, "she ain't no fool, Peg ain't. She picks the ones what ain't got no one to look out for 'em. No family, see, no one to care if you goes missing. And everyone knows that if you're on the streets you'll do almost anything to get a roof over yer head and something to fill yer belly – specially in winter. Specially *this* winter. And even if you *have* got a place – why, by the time you goes back after you bin away a few days, they're not goin' ter take yer back, are they? There's too many girls lookin' for places."

"But why does she want girls?" Megan asked fearfully. She knew Lizzie was right. Aggie would never take her back now. There was probably another girl in her place already, sharing Etty's lumpy mattress, sitting in the kitchen and peeling vegetables. And if she left Peg, what chance was there of getting another place? "What sort of work does she want you to do?"

"She makes us thieve," Lizzie said flatly. "She lets rooms and we look after the *guests*, as she calls 'em, and pinches their money and valuables. And we go out in the street and nick things – things from barrows or carts, things outa people's pockets, anything we can lay 'ands on. Then she sells 'em."

Megan sat up straight. "I won't do that! I've never stolen a thing in my life. My mam and da always brought us up to be honest—"

"Well, you won't be no more," Lizzie said bitterly. "An' you needn't think you'll get away, neither. There's bars on the front door'd keep a lion in, at the zoo. And on the windows, too. And if you don't steal nothing, she'll make it look as if you had. She'll put something on you, see – something one of her *guests*'ll miss. And she'll make sure it's found. You'll be lucky if you don't end up in jail, or deported."

"In jail? *Deported?*" Megan shook her head. "She can't do that. She *can't*."

"She's done it already," Lizzie said. "She did it to a girl she brought in not three months since. I daresay she's almost at Australia now – if she lived the journey."

Megan felt sick. She stared around the room with its armchairs, its religious paintings, its glowing range. Last night, it had seemed warm and comfortable, a haven from the bitter weather and the threats of the outside world. Now, it had turned into a prison.

"What am I going to do?" she whispered. "*What am I going to do…?*"

Chapter 29

Tom was shocked when he came back to the alehouse and discovered that Megan was missing. He put his bread-basket on the table and stared at Etty, who was scraping the mud off potatoes.

"She hasn't been here since *Tuesday*? But that's two days and nights. Where's she gone?"

Etty shrugged her thin, bony shoulders. She looked paler than ever and had to keep stopping to cough. Her eyes were enormous.

"I don't know. She said she was going to look for the girl she sang with when she first came to London. But she meant to come back that night, I know she did."

"Found herself a better place, that's what she's done," Clarrie said, piling up dirty dishes. "Found her gran, most like, and livin' in clover now. You won't see her no more."

Tom shook his head. He'd been feeling unhappy about the quarrel but had deliberately kept away from the alehouse yesterday, hoping that Megan would come round to the bakery. Now he wished he'd come before.

"She'd have come back to let us know. She wouldn't just forget us."

"Garn! She was out for number one, that one," Clarrie said scornfully. "I could see it all along. You was just bowled over by her big eyes and funny voice. Took you in proper, she did."

"She didn't at all! And there was nothing funny about her voice." She sounded as though she were singing, he thought, but he didn't say so to Clarrie. He looked at Etty.

"D'you think something's happened to her?"

"I dunno." The girl coughed again and put a rag over her mouth. As she took it away, Tom saw that it was spattered with blood. "I think she'd 'ave come back, even if she 'ad found 'er gran." She looked at Tom with big, frightened eyes. "I think something bad's happened to her."

Tom bit his lip. He thought of Megan, wandering the unfamiliar streets and alleyways in the bitter cold. Knowing nobody – perhaps lost. He thought of her spending the nights huddled in doorways, thought of what might happen to her there.

"I'll go and look for her," he said, making up his mind. "She was going to the Elephant and Castle. I'll go and find her."

Although he knew roughly where it was, Tom had never been to the Elephant and Castle before. He hurried through the streets, following almost exactly the same route as Megan had taken a few days before, but unlike Megan he didn't linger to gaze at the ice fair in Hyde Park, or watch the Changing of the

Guard at Buckingham Palace. His mind was filled with anxiety and he even crossed the Thames without pausing once to glance over the bridge at the great river flowing beneath.

Tom knew that there were many dangers lying in wait for a young girl in London. There were many people willing to take advantage of her innocence, to lead her into a life of crime, to use her for their own ends, perhaps even to hurt her – or worse. He thought of Megan falling into the hands of such people and shuddered.

And that wasn't all that might happen. She still wasn't used to the busy streets – she might step out in front of one of the big drays or a hansom cab and be run down. She might slip on the icy pavement and break her leg. Perhaps even now she was lying on a hard straw mattress, infested with fleas, in one of the city's infirmaries or workhouses, receiving the grudging care that was handed out to paupers.

Or perhaps she had fallen into the river and drowned. Or tumbled into one of the deep cuttings that were being carved out all over London for the new underground railway. Or just frozen to death in some dark, forgotten corner.

Oh Megan, Megan, he thought, why did I let you go? Why did I quarrel with you, when I should have seen just how much it meant to you?

At the corner of Brook Street and Holyoak Street, he hesitated. The high wall of the Lambeth Workhouse, stretching along the narrow pavement, made a canyon of the road, with only a strip of dirty grey cloud showing above. The street was filled with men, women and children, gaunt, grimy and ragged, who all seemed to be making for the big gates.

Tom stared at them. There was a strange wildness in their faces, a blankness in their eyes. He had seen such a look in scrawny dogs snarling over a bone, and in mangy cats as they scrabbled through mounds of rubbish in search of scraps. He had never seen it in human beings before, not even during the bread riots that had occurred outside his own father's bakery.

He stopped, half afraid to go on. The crowd took little notice of him, but he feared that if he tried to force his way through they would turn on him like the animals they resembled. He pressed himself against the wall, letting them go by, and saw in the midst of them an old man in a wheelbarrow. He looked as if he had been dropped in like a rag doll, his arms and legs flopping over the sides. His face was little more than a skull with grey, papery skin stretched tight over the bones, his nose as sharp as a beak and his eyes sunk into dark hollows. The barrow was being wheeled by a policeman, and a boy who looked almost as thin as the old man stumbled beside him.

"Clear the way, there," the policeman called. "Clear the way. We got to get this old party to the work-house. Clear the way."

Several people turned to look, and one said aggressively, "Why should we clear the way for 'im? He's goin' ter die anyway. It's us what oughter 'ave bread, not 'im."

"Bread!" some of the others started to chant, as they had done before, outside the bakery. "Bread, bread, bread!"

Their voices were harsh and desperate, voices that came from dry, starved throats. Tom could stand no more. He turned and went back, passing the workhouse gate and pausing briefly to look up at the infirmary. Could Megan be in there? He felt sick.

Once out of the crowd, he made better progress and at last he found himself on the wide road where the Elephant and Castle stood. The sign swung in the cold air, and he stopped and looked at it for a moment. You could see how it got its name, he thought. The Indian howdah looked just like a castle on the elephant's back.

His heart beat quickly. Was Megan there? Had she found her friend Sally? He lifted one hand to push open the door.

And in that very moment, he heard a sound that stilled his hand and caused him to drop it back to his side. For a full two minutes, he stood quite still, as if frozen to the spot, his head lifted and his ears straining.

Somewhere inside, a girl was singing. Her voice was sweet and pure, lifting itself like the song of a bird above all the bitterness and cares of the world. And as he listened, Tom found himself thinking of the valleys and mountains that Megan had described to him, of the streams and the bracken and the wild buzzard soaring.

The words were in Megan's language, and the melody was one he had heard on her lips.

Tom pushed open the door and went inside.

Chapter 30

Peg came in only a few minutes after Lizzie had scuttled away. She glanced sharply round the room before smiling at Megan, her eyes almost disappearing in their web of fine wrinkles.

"And how are you, my duck?" she asked in a soft, crooning voice. "Had a good sleep? You're looking better, I'll say that. I hope nobody's bin in here, disturbing you – none of them other girls, filling you up with tales?"

"No – nobody's been in," Megan said, her voice shaking a little. "What tales would they tell me?"

"Oh, nothing, nothing at all, just the silly sort of story young girls like to frighten each other with. Nothing to bother your head about. If nothing's said, no harm's done, that's what I always say." The old woman went over to the range and poked at the coals. "Now, I daresay you're ready for a cuppa tea."

A cup of tea! Megan remembered Lizzie telling her that Peg put "stuff" into the tea to make the girls sleepy. She shook her head quickly.

"I don't want any, really. I just want to go and look for my grandmother. I think I should go now – I've stayed here long enough. You've been very kind but—"

She started to get up, but Peg put her hand on her shoulder, forcing her gently back into the chair. Her small blue eyes were suspicious.

"Here, here, what's all the hurry then? I thought you'd decided to stop on here with me and the rest of my girls. I thought we were going to be pals. Are you sure nobody's been in here while I was gone?"

"No, really," Megan said desperately. "I just want to find Grandma—"

"And so you shall, my duck, so you shall." The woman's voice was crooning again. "Now, don't you get worrying yourself over your gran. We'll find her for you. Why, I've got my girls looking already, told 'em to go round the pubs and alehouses and ask for that Sally you was on about. It won't be no time at all before we've got news of her, you mark my words. Now what sense would there be in you going out in the bitter cold and the dark, not knowing where you are, when one of 'em might come in any minute and tell you just where your granny is? Eh?"

It sounded very reasonable. The "girls" would indeed have a much better chance than Megan would. And it was dark outside again, and just as icily cold. And the fire was burning up in the range, and there was a pot steaming on it that Megan hadn't noticed before. The steam smelt rich and good.

Her stomach rumbled, and she thought how little she'd had to eat lately, and how if she left here, there might be nothing...

"I still think I ought to go," she said, getting up again. "Couldn't one of the girls take me to the Elephant and Castle? If I could just find Sally – she'll remember my grandmother's address, I'm sure. And then I won't have to be any more nuisance to you."

"Bless you, childie, you're not a nuisance," Peg crooned. "Didn't I tell you you reminded me of my own little girl? Why, it warms my heart just to look at you. It's just like she'd come back to me from the dead." She moved closer and stroked Megan's cheek with her finger. "You won't leave me again, Rosie, will you? You won't leave your poor old ma all by herself again."

Megan backed away in alarm. "Don't say that! I'm not Rosie. I'm me – Megan Price. I'm *me*." She thrust her feet into her clogs and gathered up her shawl with trembling fingers. "I'm sorry – I've got to go. I've got to find Grandma—"

"*No!*" Peg screeched, and Megan jumped with fright. She stared at the old woman's face, at the mass of tiny wrinkles, at eyes that were suddenly wild and a mouth that had worked itself into a strange and frightening shape. She backed away again and felt the cold wall touch her spine. She thought of the things Lizzie had told her, and her stomach churned with fear.

Peg took a deep breath and regained control of herself. She tried to smile but her face was still distorted and the effect was grotesque. Her old eyes filled with tears.

"Please," she said, her voice soft again and quivering. "Please, duck, don't leave me. You're so much like her. I can't bear to see you go. Please..."

Megan shook her head again. "I'm sorry. I've got to. I've got my own mam to think of, and the little ones."

Peg stared at her. Slowly, her face lost its terrifying shape and began to look more normal. She held out both hands, as if begging, and after a moment's hesitation, Megan took them in her own. Perhaps it was true, she thought. Perhaps she really did remind Peg of Rosie.

"I'm sorry, duck," Peg said quaveringly. "I'm sorry. I never meant to frighten you. Course you wants to find yer gran. Course you do. It's only nat'ral, blood being thicker'n water. All I'm asking you to do is wait till tomorrow. That's reasonable, ain't it? That's sense."

It *is* reasonable, Megan thought, feeling the wrinkled hands in hers. It *is* sense. But...

"I'd rather go now," she said, trying to stop her voice shaking. "I'd really rather go now."

She looked anxiously at Peg, afraid of starting another outburst. But instead of screeching again, the old woman merely shrugged and nodded. She turned towards the door.

"Well, if that's what you want, my duck, that's what you must do. But you won't go out without something hot inside you, now will you? There's a good hot stew on the stove, all ready to serve. You'll have a bowl of that first, now won't you?"

168

Stew... It smelt delicious and Megan's empty stomach yearned for it. It was many hours since the bowl of porridge. But even as she started to say yes, the thought of the porridge stifled her words. Suppose there really had been something in it to make her sleep. Suppose Peg were to put something in the stew...

"I can't," she said. "I've got to find Grandma. I've got to go."

She could feel the panic bubbling up inside her, hear it in her voice. She tried to pass Peg to get to the door, but the old woman was in her way and wouldn't move. The panic grew.

"Please," Megan said shrilly, "*please*, let me go!"

"Let you go?" Peg said softly. "Why, of course I'll let you go, my duck. Why, I wouldn't want to keep no one here what didn't want to stay. Look, here's the door. Now you just follow me – it's dark in this passage and you might bump into something and hurt yourself."

She opened the door and vanished into the darkness. Desperate to get out, terrified now by the sinister menace of the room that had once seemed so cosy, Megan followed her. She heard Peg open another door and paused, expecting to see the brightness of a moonlit street.

"There you are," Peg said, standing aside and drawing Megan past her. "There you go, my duck. Now see if you can find your granny!"

Megan felt an unexpectedly strong hand placed

firmly between her shoulder-blades. She drew in a quick, gasping breath, but before she could cry out, the hand had pushed. She found herself lurching forwards, her feet treading on steps that weren't there, her hands reaching out blindly into pitch-dark nothingness.

The flight of steps was only short, but she landed in a crumpled heap at the bottom, every breath knocked out of her body by the fall. And above her, she heard Peg's laughter, the soft chuckle that had seemed so comfortable and now turned her blood to ice.

"And that's where you'll stay, my beauty, until you comes to your senses," the old woman hissed down the steps. "You ain't *never* going to find your granny."

The door slammed. And there was silence.

Chapter 31

The girl was plump and pretty, with dark curls that swung about her face and a red dress with a frilly, low-cut neckline and a shawl draped carelessly over her shoulders. Her lips were as red as her dress, and when she had finished her song she caught Tom's eye and smiled at him.

He made his way towards her, sat down at an empty table and ordered a pot of ale. A moment or two later, she sat down opposite him and smiled again. Her brown eyes danced with merriment.

"I ain't seen you round 'ere before."

"It's the first time I've been this way." He watched her face. "I live in Kensington."

"Kensington?" Her dark brows lifted. "What you doin' round 'ere, then?"

"I'm looking for someone." He was still watching her face, searching for clues. Surely she must be Sally. Hadn't Megan been here and found her? If not, where was she – and what had happened to her? "A Welsh girl. She sang here once, like you were doing just now."

"A Welsh girl? You mean Meg?" The girl's face lit

up. "I wondered what'd 'appened to 'er. So you know 'er, do yer? 'Ow is she? Did she find 'er granny all right?"

Tom shook his head, feeling suddenly anxious. "She's looked all over Kensington. She came back here to find you. She thought you might remember the address. D'you mean to say she hasn't been here?"

Sally shook her head. "Ain't seen 'ide nor 'air of 'er. Tell you the truth, I was a bit miffed – I thought she'd come back once she was in clover and give us a bit of an 'and, like I give 'er. But you say she never found 'er gran after all?"

"No. There's only one alehouse with 'bell' in its name in Kensington, and it certainly isn't run by her grandmother. As a matter of fact, she's been working there, but old Aggie's as mean as a crow and half-starves her servants. And without knowing the name of her grandmother's inn, there didn't seem to be any hope of finding her. That's why she came over here to find you."

"Forgot it again, did she?" Sally said with a laugh. "I dunno why she had so much trouble, it was a simple enough name. But you say she came here? Where's she got to, then?"

"That's what I'd like to know," Tom said soberly. "It was two days ago and she never came back. And she never reached the Elephant either. So what's happened to her?"

Sally's face grew grave. "Anything could've 'appened. It's a rough area round 'ere. There's some funny folk about – that's why I'd like to get out meself. And someone like Meg, who don't know London… Tell yer what, we'd better start lookin' for 'er."

"But where? We don't know where she might be – she might never have reached this area anyway." Tom shook his head, thinking of the long walk from Kensington. "She could be in Buckingham Palace, for all we know, having tea with the Queen!"

"Well, that's one place we *won't* bother lookin'," Sally declared. "Look, all we can do is our best. We'll start from 'ere and work our way back. Makes more sense than footin' it all the way back to Kensington an' startin' from there, don't it? We'll ask in all the pubs and we'll ask in the pie shops. She must've 'ad summat to eat in all that time."

"I don't think she had any money at all," Tom said hopelessly. "She could just have starved to death somewhere."

Sally gave him a sharp look. She reached across the table and patted his hand. Her eyes were soft.

"She wouldn't 'ave starved, not in two days," she said gently. "It takes a lot longer than that to starve to death – I know. I've seen it 'appen often enough." She paused and then added. "You're really worried, ain't yer? But there's summat else. Did something go wrong between you two?"

Tom stared at her. "What do you mean?"

"Well, you're sweet on 'er, ain't yer? Stands out a mile. And the way you're lookin' – well, it's as if you think it's all your fault she's disappeared. 'Ave a bit of a tiff, did yer?"

Tom felt his face grow hot. He looked away and tried to pull his hand out from under Sally's, but she held on to it and finally he looked back at her. She was smiling at him, and his embarrassment suddenly disappeared and he nodded.

"I think a lot of Meggie, yes. And we had a sort of – well, not exactly a quarrel – but she wanted to come here and I told her I couldn't, there were people waiting to be fed, starving people…" He thought of the scenes outside the workhouse. "We make bread, you see, me and my dad. I couldn't just leave it. But I didn't realize just how much it meant to Meggie."

"Ah, I see," she said, nodding. "Well, as I sees it, you were *both* right – an' there's nothing worse than two people being right in different ways! You can go round in circles for ever like that. But let's forget that for now. You've come, an' that's the main thing, specially as it seems like summat must've 'appened to stop 'er reachin' the Elephant." A sudden thought struck her. "You don't s'pose she found her gran, do you? I mean, if she'd just 'appened to run into 'er in the street, well, she wouldn't have bothered comin' 'ere at all, would she? It could be that."

"It could!" Tom said, feeling suddenly excited. Then his face fell again. "But surely she would have let me know. She knew I'd be worried about her."

"Did she?" Sally asked shrewdly, and he felt uncomfortable. *Did* Megan know how much he thought

174

of her? He'd never told her. And after that last quarrel...

Perhaps she'd thought he didn't care any more. Perhaps *she* didn't care any more...

"No," he said suddenly, "she wouldn't have just gone off without letting us know. She'd never have let Etty down, even if – well, even if she wasn't bothered about me. Something *must* have happened to her on the way here."

Sally didn't ask who Etty was. She eyed him for a moment, then shrugged and said, "Well, we'd better set about findin' 'er then. 'Ow d'you think we oughter go about it?"

"I don't know." Tom's shoulders sagged again. "It'll take weeks to ask in all the pubs and shops between here and Kensington. Months. And in that time –"

"Anything could 'appen." Sally nodded thoughtfully. "We can ask all the reg'lars, of course. And the girls what works the pubs all around. There's plenty like me, scrape together a living singin' and waitin'. Mind you, some of 'em ain't exactly welcoming to anyone new – there's only so much money to go round, and not a lot of that these days. If Meggie turned up on their doorstep, they'd likely as not send 'er off with a flea in 'er ear."

"So what do we do?" Tom asked miserably. "Stand in the middle of the road and shout?"

Sally shook her head and they sat silent for a few moments, staring at a puddle of ale that lay in the middle of the table. The serving girl came over to them, holding up her jug ready to pour into Tom's tankard, but he covered it with his hand. If there were to be a long search, he might need every penny he possessed.

"Alf says it's time you started singin' again," the girl remarked to Sally. "Says you're takin' up valuable space, and 'e don't keep a fire in to keep you warm if you ain't goin' to either pay for some beer or bring in the customers."

Sally grimaced and got to her feet. "I s'pose I'll 'ave to. I don't want to be chucked out." She looked down at Tom. "I'll come right back soon as I've finished, and you go on thinkin', mind. I liked Meg. I wouldn't want to think of 'er in trouble."

Tom nodded absently. He sipped the last of his ale and watched as Sally pushed her way to the front of the room, took up a pose in front of the old piano, and began to sing.

She had chosen another of Megan's Welsh melodies. He listened, feeling the heat of tears pricking behind his eyelids. And then he began to smile.

He knew now how to look for Megan. And if she was anywhere between Kensington and the Elephant and Castle, they would find her.

Chapter 32

Megan had no idea how long she was incarcerated in the dark, stinking little cellar. There was only a tiny grating set high in the wall to let in the dingiest scrap of light. Apart from that there was no daytime here, no dawn or dusk, not even regular meals to tell her how time was passing. Sometimes Lizzie would come down with a bowl of gruel – not the thick, nourishing soups or stews that Megan had been promised – but there was never enough to satisfy her hunger. Some of the time she slept on a pile of sacks she discovered in one corner – but whether because it was time to sleep, or because something had been put into the gruel, she had no idea. She was given a bucket for her needs, but she had no idea how often she used it, only that her stomach was cramped with pains that nothing seemed to relieve. Most of the time, she sat or lay on the sacks, or paced up and down from wall to wall – no more than six steps in either direction – and longed for escape.

Her only comfort was the little wooden doll Tom had given her at the ice fair and which she had kept in her pocket ever since. She took it out and stroked its tiny face and smoothly carved body. Would she ever see Tom again?

"Why are you keeping me here?" she asked Peg when the old woman came down once with a guttering candle. "What do you want me for?"

"What do you think?" Peg answered. "I got a business to run, ain't I? I depend on girls like you. Work for me, and I'll give you a good living. Tit-for-tat, see. That's all I ask."

"You're asking me to steal," Megan said, and Peg's eyes narrowed.

"Now, whatever give you that idea? That Lizzie bin talking? I'll tan her backside for her, see if I don't! She's always had a loose tongue."

"It wasn't her," Megan said quickly, but she knew Peg didn't believe her. "But it's true, isn't it? You make the girls steal for you. You let out rooms and they steal from your clients in the night. What I don't understand is why they don't have you arrested when they realize they've been robbed."

Peg cackled again, and Megan thought what an unpleasant sound it was. Why had she ever thought Peg's voice sounded soft and crooning?

"Didn't tell you that, did she?" Peg said. "Well, what sort of client d'you think I get round 'ere, eh? The nobs from Parlment? People what come to see the Queen and can't stop at Buck House? Scum of the earth, that's who come to stay here, my girl, and don't you make no mistake about it. Crooks, thieves, liars, the lot of 'em – and serve 'em right if they gets a dose of their own medicine. You don't have to worry yourself about *them*."

"It's stealing, just the same," Megan said obstinately. "I've always been brought up to be honest. I'm not going to be a thief for anyone."

"Suit yourself," Peg said with a shrug, and blew out the candle. Its feeble light died and the cellar was once more as black as pitch, before a shred of dim light struggled though the grating. "Another week or two down here and you might be ready to change your mind. It's never failed yet."

Megan heard her go up the steps and slam the door again. The shadows closed about her again, the darkness like something solid, pressing against her from all sides.

She drew her knees up to her chin and wrapped her arms around her legs. As well as being dark, the cellar was very cold. She had spent hours last night, jumping up and down until she was exhausted, in an effort to keep warm. She tucked her freezing fingers into her armpits and huddled closer into her sacks.

I shouldn't ever have come to London, she thought. I shouldn't ever have left the valley. Morgan was right – I ought to have stayed at home and done as he wanted. At least I could be a bit of help to Mam. Now I'm no help at all.

She wondered what was happening back in Kensington. Had Aggie taken on another girl to help in the kitchen? Had she found someone to go on with the singing, to bring customers in? Or had she been forced to close her doors, like the many shops and alehouses Megan had seen with doors and windows boarded while their owners skulked inside, living on whatever was left?

What would Etty do if such a thing happened? Megan knew Aggie well enough to realize that she would feel no responsibility for the sick girl. If she helped her to get to the workhouse, she would feel that she had been kinder than anyone had a right to expect. And how long would Etty last in that dreaded place?

And what of Tom? Had he been so hurt and annoyed by Megan's ingratitude that he had simply washed his hands of her? Perhaps he thought it was good riddance.

Perhaps he was taking Clarrie to the ice fair now.

Megan's tears felt hot – the only warmth she had in her body now. They dripped on to her skirt and soaked through the worn material on to her knees. A long, shuddering sob forced its way up from her chest.

Outside, through the grating, she could hear the sounds of the street – the clop of horses' hooves, the footsteps of people passing by. At first, she had tried shouting for help, but nobody had taken any notice. Cries and shouts were commonplace in these dingy streets, and everyone was too busy struggling for their own survival to take note of someone else's problems. Besides, you could find yourself in worse trouble if you interfered. Why, only last week a man had been killed – stabbed and beaten to death – for going to the help of an old woman being set upon by thugs.

Megan sat listening, her despair greater than it had ever been. Out there were people who, though poor and starving, were at least free to walk the streets, while she was imprisoned in this terrible dank dungeon, not knowing whether she would ever see the light of day again. And if she were set free, it would be to thieve for the old woman who had trapped her here.

I won't, she thought. I *won't*.

But if she didn't…?

A sound from outside made her lift her head sharply – a sound she hadn't heard before, rising as pure as the song of a lark above the rattle of vehicles, the clatter of hooves and the street cries of the few traders who were left. A sound that took her soul winging back to the mountains and valleys of her beloved homeland.

> *Gwlad, gwlad, pleidiol wyf i'm gwlad,*
> *Tra mor yn fur*
> *I'r bur hoff bau,*
> *O bydded i'r heniaith barhau.*

Megan caught her breath. She sat as taut as a spring, straining to hear the verse repeated. Perhaps it had been a dream – a delusion. She'd heard that such things happened to people who were slowly dying of cold and starvation. Was this what was happening to her? Oh, let it be repeated!

181

The voice came again.

Gwlad, gwlad, pleidiol wyf i'm gwlad...

Megan jumped up. She tumbled over to the grating and stretched herself towards it, then lifted her voice in reply.

Tra mor yn fur
I'r bur hoff bau...

And heard, with amazement and incredulity, the other voice join in the song, so that their two voices rose together, and dipped on the last, plaintive note.

O bydded i'r heniaith barhau...

There was a brief pause. Then she heard another voice – a male voice this time, one that she scarcely dared think she recognized. But he was calling her name: "Megan! Megan! Is it you? Oh Meggie, say it's you! Say it's you for God's sake!"

"Tom?" she whispered. "Tom?"

His voice was close to the grating now.

"Meggie, where are you? Call more loudly."

"I can't." She was panic-stricken. "She'll hear me. I'm in the cellar. She's locked me in. She wants me to steal for her. Oh Tom, Tom, get me out of here – please, *please* get me out..." She was sobbing now, terrified by the need to keep quiet yet unable to stop her voice rising with her tears. Outside, she could hear a whispered consultation. Who did he have with him? Who had been singing that song? "Tom, help me, please help me…"

"It's all right, Meg." Of course – it was Sally's voice. Sally was the only girl who knew that song, who knew what it would mean to Megan. "We'll get you out. She can't do anything to you now that we know you're here."

Megan wasn't so sure. To her, Peg had begun to seem like a witch, with frightening and unnatural powers. Suppose she lured Sally and Tom into the cellar and locked them in, as she had done with Megan? What would they do then?

She crawled back to her pile of sacks and huddled there, listening. She could hear nothing from the house above. The floor was as solid as a rock and for all she knew the house could have been empty all the time. What was happening? Had Tom and Sally gone for a policeman? If so, how long would it be before they came back? Would the police believe them?

"Get away from that door, blast you!"

The voice sounded almost in her ear, at the top of the cellar steps. It was Peg's screech, the screech that was so different from her soft, crooning tones. She sounded savagely angry and Megan cringed against the wall. At any moment she expected the door to fly open and both Tom and Sally to come hurtling down the steps to land beside her, captives like herself.

The door flew open, just as she'd expected. Two figures came hurtling down the steps. But they did not land in crumpled heaps on the floor and the door wasn't slammed behind them. Instead, one of them scooped her up into his arms, while the other took one disgusted glance around and dragged a third figure down after her, tossing it on the floor like a heap of rags.

"There!" Sally said in tones of rich satisfaction. "Take a dose of yer own medicine. I'll tell them poor girls you bin treatin' like slaves to give yer just what yer bin givin' poor Meggie here. Bowl of gruel twice a day, was it? An' a bucket in the corner? Well, if it's good enough for Meg, it's twice too good for you, but we'll let yer keep it, just outa the kindness of our 'earts – won't we, Tom?"

"Just leave her there," he growled from the top of the steps, where he had carried Megan. "Leave her there and come up out of it. Lizzie'll look after her – while she feels like it."

He turned and marched along the dark, narrow passage and into the street. Megan blinked, startled by the brightness of the daylight. She drew in a quick gasp of surprise.

At some time during her imprisonment it must have snowed, and everything was white and glittering. A soft blanket had been flung over the streets, covering tumbledown buildings and sagging roofs with billows as dimpled as an eiderdown and hiding their broken tiles and crumbling walls. This was what it might have looked like years ago, Megan thought, before it all began to decay.

But there was no time to think of that now. Lizzie was standing on the pavement with half a dozen other girls. They all looked thin and pale, and their clothes were ragged. Megan knew that they had all been forced to work for Peg, as she herself would have been forced, and that they were as trapped as she had been. There was nowhere for a girl to go in London when she had no home and no work, but to these decaying tenements where the lowest of all human forms lurked and crawled and used one another for their own survival.

"She's in the cellar," Tom said to the girls. "Do whatever you like with her. We're not bothered."

The girls glanced at each other. They looked up at the house with its crumbling walls and rotting timbers. They looked at each other again, and began to smile.

"All that grub in the pantry…" Lizzie said.

"All that money she's got hid away…" said another.

"All them trinkets and stuff…" whispered a third, and with one movement they turned and fled back into the house.

Tom laughed. "They'll be all right. And old Peg'll fare better than she deserves — they won't let her starve. And now," he looked down into Megan's face, "let's get you somewhere warm and put some food inside you. And then we'll see about finding your granny."

Chapter 33

They went to Sally's room, to the dank little cellar she was so proud of just because it was hers. On the way, Tom bought some hot pies and a bottle of ale, and they lit a fire in the tiny grate and sat close together around it. Megan was shivering, great shudders that ran over her body in waves, and the other two sat one on each side, their arms about her in an effort to give her warmth.

"It's the shock," Sally said wisely. "It's a reaction. That woman oughter be flogged, keepin' you down that hole. Eat your pie, Meg. You'll feel better with some food inside yer."

"I can't. I thought I was hungry, but I can't swallow it."

"Just take a little bit at a time," Sally advised. "Don't rush. It'll give you strength to eat the rest."

Slowly, Megan nibbled at the pie and found that Sally was right. A morsel of flaky crust and the thick, hot juice inside seemed to give her the energy for another bite. Soon she had finished the whole pie and drunk some ale, and was feeling better.

"There, that's the ticket," Sally said approvingly.

"Got a bit of colour in yer cheeks now. Soon be right as ninepence."

Megan gave her a wavery smile and then turned to Tom.

"How did you come to be with Sally? How did you find each other?"

"I looked," he said with a grin. "I knew you were coming to the Elephant so I followed you. I heard Sally singing in Welsh and knew she must be the girl you'd known. I thought you'd have found her before me – it was a nasty shock when I discovered that you hadn't even arrived at the Elephant." His face grew sober. "Meggie, I'm sorry about what happened. I should never have let you go off on your own. When I think about what might have happened if we hadn't found you—" He shuddered.

"It's all right," Megan said quietly. "You were right. I saw so many hungry people on my way here. And I know what it is to be hungry, too. I've never been so starved as I was in that cellar – and it was only for a few days. To go on like that, day after day… People need your bread, Tom. You shouldn't be bothering about me when there's people dying for want of it."

"I can't help bothering about you," he said in a low voice, and they sat silent for a moment, forgetting their troubles, forgetting Megan's search, content just to be together.

"If you two don't mind," Sally said suddenly, in a loud voice, "we can't sit 'ere all day moonin'. You got a granny to find, ain't yer? I s'pose she *does* still live in

London — she ain't gone somewhere else?"

"Yes, she does!" Megan exclaimed, remembering. "We saw her in Hyde Park, didn't we, Tom? We would have caught up with her, only I fell and sprained my ankle. But I know she's here somewhere." She looked at Sally with excitement in her eyes. "That's why I was looking for you — to see if you could remember the name of her inn. You see, I lost the piece of paper — it was in my purse, and it was stolen before I had a chance to start searching. And I could never remember that name, only that there was a bell in it—"

"Lost the piece of paper?" Sally repeated, staring at her. "But that was never pinched. It wasn't even in your purse. *I* 'ad it! I pushed it into me pocket that day you were 'ere, and it wasn't till after you'd gone that I found it. I thought you'd come back for it — I never thought of you losin' yer purse and thinkin' it'd bin inside."

"*You* had it?" Megan said in astonishment. "But — but why didn't you come and find me?"

"Why didn't *you* come and find *me*?" Sally retorted. "You knew where I was if you wanted me. Wasn't for me to come buttin' in, was it now? When you never come back, I thought you'd found yer granny and gone back to Wales and I wasn't never goin' to see you no more. I didn't know you'd forgot the address again."

Megan fell silent. Sally was perfectly right. There was no reason why she should come looking for a girl she had met once, helped out and wished goodbye. It had been for Megan to make the approach and perhaps repay the help Sally had given her.

"Can you still remember the address?" she asked, without much hope. "If you could just tell me its name, so that I could find Grandma – and I wouldn't go off and leave you, Sally. Not after all you've done for me."

"Remember it? I don't need to remember it." Sally laughed at Megan's downcast face. "Don't look so miserable, Meg. I still got the paper, ain't I? I've kept it all the time." She fished in her pocket and brought out the scrap of paper that Megan had brought all the way from Wales. "'Ere you are. *You* tell *me* what it is!"

Megan took the paper in trembling fingers. She unfolded it, saw the familiar scrawl. As she gazed at it, Tom looked over her shoulder and read it aloud.

"Mrs Coleman, The Twelve Bells, Ken—" He stopped suddenly. "Meggie, look at that! Don't you see what it says? The Twelve Bells, *Kennington*! It's not Kensington at all. You've been looking in the wrong part of London all along!"

Chapter 34

"Kennington?" Megan repeated wonderingly. "I didn't even know there was such a place." She looked at Sally. "Have you heard of it?"

"'Eard of it? Course I 'ave – it's only just round the corner from 'ere. Well, a mile or so away I s'pose as the crow flies. I don't go there much, so I don't know this pub, but I daresay it's there right enough."

Tom looked at her. "You've had this piece of paper all this time. You must have looked at it when Meggie first showed it to you. Didn't you notice the name then?"

Sally looked half embarrassed, half defiant. "No, I didn't. I can't read, can I? It don't mean nothing to me – just a lot of squiggles. I wouldn't even know the place was called the Twelve Bells if it didn't 'ave a sign with bells on."

"Well, we know now," Megan said, unable to keep the excitement out of her voice. "And if it isn't far away, why not go at once? She might be there at this very minute." She was on her feet, pulling at their arms. "Come *on* – what are we waiting for?"

Sally laughed. "Well, that's put the roses back, an'

no mistake. Look at 'er, Tom. Would you think it was the same girl?"

Tom looked at Megan and smiled. But there was still a doubt in his face. He laid his hand briefly on Megan's shoulder.

"Wait there a minute."

The girls watched uncertainly as he went up the narrow steps that led out of the cellar into the dark, narrow passage, and opened the front door. They felt the blast of cold air that swirled in from the street outside, and heard him shut the door again hastily. He came back down the steps.

"We won't be going anywhere for a while," he said quietly. "There's a real blizzard out there. You can't see your hand in front of your face. We're going to have to wait till it stops before we stir an inch."

The blizzard continued for two days and nights. Several times Tom went out to buy food, but as the hours went by he came back looking glummer each time, reporting that the pie shops were running low, the bakeries closed and hardly anything available. Until the storm had passed, there was nothing anyone could do.

"And no fuel to be had either," he said, putting the last of their small store of coal on to the tiny fire. "The coal barges have been frozen in on the canals and rivers for weeks now, and with the snow so deep it can't be transported by road. It's terrible out there."

He didn't mention the people he had seen, the

homeless and starving, freezing to death in doorways and alleys. The snow-covered humps that nobody had the energy to uncover. The girls would see those soon enough, when they were finally able to emerge from the cellar.

"What must your mam and dad be thinking?" Megan asked worriedly. "You've been gone for three days now. They must be almost out of their minds."

"I told them where I was coming," he reassured her. "I said I'd not be back until I'd found you. And they'll know I couldn't cross London in this weather."

But he knew they would still be anxious, especially his mother. If only there were some way to let them know he was safe.

For the rest of the night, the three of them huddled together, drawing warmth from each other's bodies. There was little sleep, but they dozed for part of the time and once Megan woke to find herself wrapped closely in Tom's arms. It was a strange sensation, reminding her sharply of her babyhood when her mother or father had held her, and she felt again that same, secure comfort. Yet there was a difference: this was Tom, not her father, and she was no longer a baby.

She thought about it for a few moments, dreamily watching the last of the flickering light from the dying flames. Then she closed her eyes again in contentment, and slept.

It was morning when she woke again. A wisp of light drifted in through the cracks around the hatch which was the cellar's only glimpse of the outside world. A wisp of bright, white light…

"It's stopped snowing," Tom said as she stirred. "It's stopped snowing, and the sun's come out."

For a few moments they sat close, thinking of the days that had passed and the ones that were to come. It had been a strange time, a time of companionship and growing closeness, when the world had seemed to contract to just this tiny cellar and the three of them. There had been cold and discomfort, hunger and anxiety, yet through it all Megan was aware that something precious had taken place, something she would never forget. Something that would stay with her and support her for the rest of her life…

Sally moved and sat up. The dim light filtered through to show her face, puzzled and half awake. Then she saw Tom and Megan and smiled.

"It's daytime."

"Yes, it's daytime," Tom said, "and time we were on our way. We've a grandmother to find."

Sally jumped to her feet and pushed the hatch aside to peer out. Light flooded in and they saw the snow piled up on the pavement, a cliff of glistening white at least two feet deep. Outside they could hear the sounds of people talking, of snow being scraped from the road. Traders were beginning to urge their horses through the streets; food must be brought to the hungry people, coals hauled from the frozen rivers and canals. The city was anxious to be moving again.

"We won't bother with breakfast," Sally said with a wry humour, for there was no food left in the cellar, nor any fuel. But they hardly cared now, for the sky was clear and blue, and the beauty of the snow had transformed the dinginess of the city. Roads that were normally roughly cobbled and thick with mire were now smooth fairways of gleaming white. Rooftops that were usually bowed and sagging now had the higgledy-piggledy look of a nursery rhyme illustration, while above them the spires and domes of churches rose like a fantasy of shimmering icicles.

"I've never seen anything so beautiful," Megan said in an awed whisper. "Not even in Wales!"

"And that's saying something," Tom remarked, taking both girls' arms. "Come on. It's not far to Kennington, but it'll be hard walking in this snow. The sooner we start, the better."

It was hard walking, and soon their toes were frozen, but the thought that their quest might soon be at an end buoyed up their spirits and kept them moving. They soon realized that the beauty of the snow had done nothing to diminish the squalor and hardships of the streets through which they trudged. It simply hid them under a blanket of shining innocence – the kind of innocence to be seen on the face of a young boy recently taken to crime. Beneath it lay all the suffering that there had been before it fell, and more.

"It isn't right," Megan said passionately as they passed the workhouse and saw the gaunt faces staring from the windows and the thin figures moving slowly about the yards, scraping feebly at the snow while the warders bullied them to work harder. "It isn't right that some people should be so poor while others are so rich. We all work hard. We should share everything equally."

She thought of Queen Victoria in her grand coach, of the well-fed people she had seen on her way through the city. Even in this bitter winter, there were still people who had enough to eat and warm clothes to wear. Yet there were thousands of others with no homes, no food or money, with only rags to wrap around their freezing bodies.

"Maybe one day we will," Tom said. "There are movements afoot … unions and societies to help the common people. Maybe one day it'll all be put right."

They walked in silence for a while. The snow was up to their knees, making each step an effort. Yet it was so light that it drifted away, like a fine white powder, as they lifted their feet.

"It's so strange," she said after a minute or two. "We're in Kennington Road now – I actually walked a little way along here when I first came to Lambeth, before I met Peg. If only I'd known…"

"You might have got lost anyway, and we'd never have found you," Tom finished with a grin. "And now I reckon we'd better ask someone. Kennington's a big place and we don't want to be wandering around here when it gets dark again."

The first two people they asked shook their heads. They were strangers here themselves, they said. But the third screwed up his face when they asked for the

Twelve Bells and scratched his head as if he was sure he knew it, if only it would come to mind.

"Lessee, ain't that down Claylands Road? No, I tell a lie – that's the *Ring* o' Bells. I know that 'cause I got a mate lives near there an' we bin in for a sup of ale now an' then. The *Twelve* Bells – I know it, know it as well as I know me own name. It's – it's – no, don't tell me," he said, as if Tom and Megan and Sally were about to shout the answer at him. "It's in Upper Kennington Lane, that's where it is, on the corner of Harleyford Road, what leads down to the Oval." He beamed triumphantly. "You just keep goin', you can't miss it."

He went on his way as happy as if he had just passed an examination, and Tom and the two girls looked excitedly at each other and set off again, scarcely noticing the snow or the cold of their toes, or even the darkening sky. It could only be a matter of minutes now, surely, before they were inside the Twelve Bells, toasting their toes before a roaring fire, sipping tankards of spicy mulled ale and being fussed over by Megan's grandmother who, Megan had assured them, was the kindest person in the world.

And indeed it looked as if their dream were to come true. For within a quarter of an hour, they had reached the junction of Upper Kennington Lane and Harleyford Road. And there before them, its sign swinging in the cold air, and plainly illustrated with twelve bells, so that even Sally could not have doubted it, stood the Twelve Bells.

196

They stared at it. And Megan's heart sank.

The windows were boarded and blank. The door was barred. It was clear that the inn was firmly closed and that nobody lived there any more. The stone-battered boards and the scarred door showed that it had been empty for quite a long time.

"Oh *Grandma*," Megan said, and in her voice could be heard the breaking of her heart, "what's happened to you? Where are you now?"

Chapter 35

"So what are you going to do next?" Mrs Bradley asked.

Megan and Sally were sitting at the kitchen table in the bakehouse, eating one of Mrs Bradley's famous pies. Tom had had his dinner and gone back to work. Since their return hardly any work had been done, for everyone had wanted to hear their adventures, but at last Mr Bradley had reminded them that there was bread to be made and the men had all gone back to their troughs of dough and their long wooden tables. They could be heard now, thumping the dough as they kneaded it.

"Oh, I shall go and look for Grandma as soon as Tom has time to come with me," Megan said. "He's made me promise I won't go again by myself, though I'm sure I could find my way, and Sally—"

"Tom's right," Mrs Bradley said firmly. "We don't want you wandering off again and getting yourself lost. Anyway, London's no place these days for a girl on her own – no, nor two neither," she added as Sally began to protest. "I don't care how long you've lived in the city, nor how long you've looked after yourself.

There's a lot of desperate people about, and you don't know what might happen next with all these bread riots and so on."

Megan went on eating her pie. Since coming back to the bakery, she had appreciated Mrs Bradley's cooking all the more. Plain bread was joy enough, but a pie, with real meat and gravy under a topping of crisp flaky pastry, was like ambrosia. She ate slowly, savouring every mouthful as she thought of what had happened since they had turned the corner of Upper Kennington Lane to find the Twelve Bells firmly closed.

It had been the worst moment Megan had known yet. To have come so far on her search, to arrive at what she had expected to be her grandmother's door and find it barred against her, with no sign that Grandma had ever been there... It was almost too much. After that first despairing appeal, she had turned away, convinced that she had wasted her time, that she would never find her grandmother and might as well have stayed in Wales.

"Megan!" Tom had been beside her in an instant, his arm around her shoulders. "Megan, don't cry. I'm sure this is the right place. All we need to do now is—"

"There's *nothing* we can do!" She'd looked up into his face, her eyes enormous. "She's gone, you can see that – if she was ever here at all. She's gone, and now I'll never find her."

"You will. *We* will. We'll ask everyone if they know where she's gone. We'll find out everything we can about her – ask the neighbours, the customers who used to come here, the brewer who supplied beer. Someone will know where she is."

"It could take weeks," Megan had said hopelessly. "Months. And poor Mam, back in Wales – I can't stay away for ever Tom. They need me."

He'd looked at her very seriously and she'd thought he was about to say something. But whatever it was, he'd bitten it back and instead said quietly, "It doesn't matter how long it takes, Megan. We'll find her. And if you have to go back to Wales, then I'll go on looking. She's in London somewhere, we know it – we've *seen* her."

Megan had felt a touch of warmth and hope. For a few minutes, she had forgotten that sight of her grandmother that she had had in Hyde Park. Tom was right. She was in London somewhere, and surely they were better off now than they had been before, for they had found the address she had given Megan's mother.

And in fact it had taken no time at all to discover where Bronwen Coleman had gone. A Welshwoman was easily remembered in these streets where the harsh tones of the Cockney accent were most often heard, and there were plenty of people who remembered Arthur Coleman and his wife. The Twelve Bells had been a popular alehouse until the lease ran out, Megan was told, and everyone had been sorry when it was closed.

"Took some of my best custom with it, too," the local baker had said. It had been Tom's idea to go there, for wouldn't a baker have supplied bread to everyone in the area? "Those that can afford to eat now – and they're not much more common than hens' teeth these days – go down the King's Head in Fentiman Road, and he gets his bread from Parker's."

"But where did she go?" Megan had asked impatiently. She couldn't bear to stand there listening to a lot of grumbles about hard times and lost trade, not now, when she was so close to finding her grandmother. "Did she tell you where she was going?"

"Arthur Coleman did," the baker had said, as if the innkeeper's wife didn't have a tongue. "Said they were going up Hampstead way. Done good business round here so they were investing in a better place. Said his wife hankered for fresh air, didn't like the city streets."

"Hampstead!" Megan had turned to Tom. "Where's that? Is it in the country?"

"Almost. There's a heath there – a stretch of open land, all grass and trees. They have fairs there sometimes. I went once – it's just like being in the countryside. And there are big houses there. People with money. If your gran's gone there, she must be doing well."

Megan had turned back to the baker. "Did she – did Arthur Coleman tell you their new address? Is it another inn?"

"Hotel, that's what they said." The baker had laid his finger on his top lip and lifted his head with a sniff. "Too good for the likes of Kennington folk. Mind, they were a decent couple, never put on airs. I don't grudge 'em their luck."

"So what is it? The address?" Megan had been hardly able to stand still. She'd jigged from foot to foot and had only just managed to restrain herself from leaning across the baker's counter and grabbing him by the throat. "What's the name of their hotel?"

"Didn't I tell you? It's a funny sort of name – not sure I can remember." He'd scratched his head, while Megan almost screamed with impatience. "Let's see, was it the Mucky Duck?" He'd grinned and she'd realized he was teasing her. "No, that wasn't it. The Swan – the *Black* Swan – that's what it was. The Black Swan, East Heath Road, that's where they went. Arthur and Bronwen Coleman, The Black Swan, East Heath Road, Hampstead. There!" He'd beamed at them, as proud as a puppy which had just achieved a clever trick.

For a second or two, Megan had felt like reaching across and patting him on the head. Instead, she'd leaned over and kissed his cheek.

"Thank you! Oh, *thank* you. Oh, that's wonderful. At last we know where she is. We'll go there straight away." She'd turned to Tom and Sally, her face alight. "We can, can't we? I can't bear to waste any more time." She'd set off out of the bakery.

"Hold your horses," Tom had said, grinning back, as pleased as if it had been his own grandmother they had been searching for. "We can't go there today. It'll be dark soon for a start, and it's right in the opposite direction – miles from here. We'll have to go home first – back to Kensington. For one thing, I ought to let my mum and dad know where I am. And—"

"Oh Tom," Megan had exclaimed guiltily, "of course you must. How could I have forgotten? They'll be so worried. And I must see how Etty is. But then? Then can we go?"

"We'll go the first minute we can," Tom had promised, taking her hand. "But now we've got to go home. We can't risk being out in the streets when it starts to get dark, and look at the sky – I wouldn't be surprised if there's more snow on the way."

Megan had looked up and shivered. The clouds were massing overhead again, thick and yellow like bruises in the sky. A cold wind was whipping through the streets, sending flurries of snow into the air. She'd seen a solitary flake, as big as a guinea, come floating slowly down.

"But what shall I do?" she'd asked. "I don't suppose Aggie will take me back. And Sally – I can't bear to think of Sally going back to that horrible cellar."

Tom had smiled at her. "You'll stop with us, of course. And Sally too," he'd added, turning to the dark girl who was standing a little apart, looking oddly lonely. "We'd never have got this far without her; we can't leave her behind now."

"I won't say I wouldn't be glad to come," Sally had said, "but I've got a living to earn. I don't want to leave my regular place and find someone else has took it when I gets back."

"There'll be a place for you at Kensington," Tom had declared. "Mum was saying the other day she could do with a girl to help her round the place. I thought of Meggie – but if she finds her gran, she won't need us." He'd turned away as he spoke, his voice slightly muffled. "Anyhow, you could do with a good meal inside you and a warm, if nothing else. So you come back with us."

And now here they were, sitting at Mrs Bradley's kitchen table and eating as if they had not seen food for a month. And indeed it felt like a month, Megan thought, for despite the food Tom had brought while they were in Sally's cellar, they had never been really satisfied. And the long walk back from Kennington had sharpened their appetites even more.

She finished her pie and smiled at Mrs Bradley.

"Well, there's still one thing I must do before I go anywhere else," she said. "I must go to Aggie's and see how Etty is. And when I do find Grandma, I'll ask if she can take Etty in." Her face grew sad. "I don't think it would be for long. I don't think she'll ever see winter again."

"I think you're right," Mrs Bradley said. "But we won't wait for you to find your grandmother. Tom'll go straight round this minute and fetch Etty back here. You can share a bed in the little room next to the bakehouse, where the nightworkers sometimes take a rest. It's not very big, but it's warm."

"And tomorrow," Tom said, poking his head round the door to say goodnight, "we'll go to Hampstead, and this time we really *will* find your grandmother!"

Chapter 36

"We're here," Megan said softly. "The Black Swan. Oh, please, *please* let Grandma be here…"

East Heath Road ran along the edge of the Heath. To Megan, it was the nearest she had seen to real country-side since leaving the valleys. A wide expanse of snow, dotted with frosted shrubs and trees, stretched before her and to one side she could see the shimmer of ice, with skaters swooping like butterflies between the banks. It wasn't like the mountains of South Wales, but at least there were no oppressive streets crowding in upon her, no towering soot-blackened walls, no snivelling, half-starved children in the gutter or beggars stretching out trembling claws in desperate appeal.

"It's real country," Sally said in awe. "Like a proper village. You wouldn't think there was all that just behind you, in the city."

It had taken them quite a long time to travel out to Hampstead. For part of the way they had come by horse bus, but then they had started to walk. It was midday when they finally stood at the door of the Black Swan.

"Looks a well set-up place," Tom remarked, glancing at the front of the building. "Been looked after – you can see that by the paintwork and the wood. Not a touch of rot, see? And that sign's been freshly painted, too, by a good craftsman. I'd say—"

"For Gawd's sake, Tom," Sally interrupted, "we ain't come to buy the place! All we want to know is whether Meg's gran lives 'ere. Let's cut the cackle and go inside, shall we, before I take root on the pavement."

Megan laughed. She was trembling with excitement, but she'd been strangely relieved to stand for a few moments outside the inn, just gathering her courage to venture inside. This was the last stage of a quest which had proved more difficult than she had expected. She was almost afraid to move, in case it should prove just one more bitter disappointment.

If I don't find Grandma now, she thought, I don't think I'll have the heart to carry on. And she stood as if in a trance, unable for a moment to take that one last step.

But Sally's words brought her back to reality. It had started to snow again and they were all cold from the journey. She smiled at them both, took a deep breath and pushed open the door.

The warm air enveloped them as if someone had gathered them into a welcoming embrace, and the first thing they saw was a log fire in a huge brick hearth. Big leather armchairs were drawn up round the hearth, and wooden settles stood against the walls. Over in the corner was a bar, gleaming with bottles and glasses, and a row of pewter tankards hanging above it reflected the glimmering firelight. Behind the bar was a tall man, with curly hair as grey as iron, that spread round his ruddy cheeks and smiling mouth into a springing beard. He looked at the three travellers and tilted his head to one side.

"Well, you're a welcome sight on a cold morning. I was beginning to think nobody was coming today. What'll it be, a glass of mulled ale or a sip of warm ginger wine?"

"Either sounds just the ticket," Tom said, advancing towards him. "But there's something else we want from you first. It's all right," he added hastily as the man's eyes narrowed with suspicion, "we aren't here to rob you. We just want to know if you're Arthur Coleman, late of the Twelve Bells at Kennington, and if you're married to Bronwen Coleman who used to be Price?"

The man continued to look suspicious. "Who wants to know?"

Before Tom could speak again, Megan pushed past him and ran up to the bar. Her face was flushed, her eyes aglow, and she looked prettier than Tom had ever seen her. She gazed up into Arthur Coleman's eyes.

"Mr Coleman! Don't you know me? I'm Megan – Megan Price. Your wife's my grandma. Is she here? Please say yes – I've come so far to find her. *Is* she?"

Arthur Coleman stared at her. He reached out and touched her cheek wonderingly, as if to assure himself she was real.

"Megan. Little Megan. So it *was* you we saw that

day on the ice. Bron swore it was, but the minute she'd set eyes on you, you vanished in the crowd and we could never find you after that. Well, we had no idea where to look, did we? And she's been that worried, thinking what might have happened to you. But here you are, safe and sound." He beamed. "And your grandma'll be back any minute now – she just popped out for a minute or two."

The street door opened. It brought with it a flurry of snowflakes. And it brought also a small, plump woman wearing a thick cloak and a warm bonnet, with grey curls peeping out around its edges. A woman who took one look at the little group round the fireplace and then ran forward with a cry of gladness.

"Megan! It's really you! Oh *cariad*, how did you come here? I've been looking out for you these past four weeks or more, thinking you must be lost. And London's a bad place to be lost in, a bad, bad place."

She pushed the others aside and knelt beside the sofa, pulling Megan against her bosom. The soft warmth of her was all around, her affection like a downy comfort that filled the air.

"Where have you been, you bad girl?" she chided gently. "What are you doing here? It's a long way from the valleys. And how is everyone at home? There's nothing wrong, I hope?"

Megan gazed at her. Bronwen Coleman hadn't written since she'd left the Rhondda. She didn't know about Morgan Jones, she didn't even know her son Owen had been killed.

"Oh Grandma," she said sadly, "there's such a lot to tell you…"

It took a long time to tell, but at last it was over and they sat silent around the fire. They had moved out of the public bar into the living-room where Arthur and Bron had their own quarters, and they had been given bowls of hot stew and mugs of spiced ale. But the story Megan had to tell was a cold one, and Bron Coleman shivered as she looked into the fire and tried to come to terms with the news that her son was dead.

"I wrote," she said sorrowfully. "I wrote several times. But I never had an answer. I thought maybe he was angry with me for marrying again and moving to London… If only I'd known…"

"The letters never came," Megan said. "And Mam wrote to you after the accident, but we never heard and she thought you didn't care. But after Morgan Jones came into the house, I knew I had to find you. You're the only person who can help."

"And help I will," Bron declared. "I'll go straight away – and you must come with me, Megan. Your poor mam must be worried out of her mind. We'll see what can be done. She doesn't have to stay with that man. If she wants to come away, I'll bring her back to London with me. I can't leave her and my grand-children under the thumb of a creature like that, indeed I can't. We'll find some way out of it for her."

She looked determined. And Megan and Tom looked

at each other and smiled. Nobody, they thought, would be able to stand up to this plump little grandmother when her eyes flashed and her mouth was set in just that way. Not even Morgan Jones.

Chapter 37

After London, the villages of the Rhondda seemed small and cramped. Stepping down from the train with her grandmother and Arthur Coleman, Megan stared about her with surprise. Only the mountains, looming above, seemed as big as she remembered.

"I must have got used to the streets and big buildings without realizing it," she said. But she was too eager to see her mother and the family again to linger, and they hurried along the narrow roads to the house where Megan had grown up. "Oh, I hope everyone's all right. It seems so long since I saw them."

As she turned the last corner she felt as if her heart would leap from her chest, it was beating so hard. She clutched her grandmother's hand tightly. And then they were at the door. Her fingers trembling, she lifted the latch and pushed.

They were all there, sitting round the table – Mam, Owen, Dafydd, Emlyn, Bronwen and Gwen. They had steaming bowls in front of them and as Megan pushed open the door they turned and stared. Then Dilys came to her feet with a cry and ran to fling her arms around her daughter.

"Oh Mam! Mam!" Megan cried, the tears pouring down her cheeks. The other children were gathered round too, each vying to hug her. She tried in vain to get her arms around them all at once and they stood in a laughing, weeping huddle in the doorway, everyone talking at once, asking questions and not waiting for the answers.

"Where have you been, *cariad*?" "Is it true you went to London?" "It's been so cold here, you'd never believe it." And then Owen's voice, incredulous, "Why, there's *Grandma*!"

Dilys let Megan go. She looked past her daughter at the couple standing behind her. Her tear-streaked face crumpled again and she reached out blindly to her mother-in-law.

"Mam. I thought we were never going to see you again."

Bron Coleman held her closely. Her own eyes were brimming with tears. Softly, she said, "I thought you'd taken offence that I went away. I wrote – often – but Megan says you never got my letters. And I never got yours either."

"We found out why," Owen said. "Old Evans the Post had been stealing the stamp money. He just pushed all the letters into an old mine up the mountain and spent it in the alehouse. They've deported him now, to Australia."

"So you didn't know..." Dilys began, her eyes on Bron's face.

"About my Owen? Megan told me." Bron looked

past the family to the room beyond. "She told me about Morgan Jones too. Where is he?"

Dilys glanced away. "He died. He caught pneumonia a month ago. I nursed him as well as I could – but he wasn't a well man, you know."

"He was a scrounger," Megan said bluntly. "And I'm not sorry he's dead. You're better off without him, Mam."

They all came indoors and sat round the fire. The family had been sitting down to a dinner of thick soup, and Dilys insisted that it be shared with the three new-comers. "We're a bit better off now," she said. "The mines are working again after the winter and even the little ones can earn a few pence at the pit-head. And I must admit that without Morgan to feed –"

"And keep in drink," Megan muttered.

"– things do seem a little bit easier." She looked at Megan. "I've missed you sorely, though, *cariad*. I don't think I've had a night's sleep since you went, worrying about what might have happened."

"Well, I'm safe, as you can see." Megan knew she would never tell her mother all that had happened to her in London. "And now Grandma's here too, and everything will be all right."

Bron smiled. "It's up to you, of course, Dilys," she said. "You're free to make up your own mind what to do. But Arthur and me, we'd like to put a proposition to you." She drank some soup appreciatively. "You're a good cook, always have been, and a good house-keeper too."

"I had good training up at the big house," Dilys said.

"I know. And what we thought was that now the mines are open again and doing well, we might set you up in a small hostelry here, the sort I ran myself, where the mine managers could entertain business guests. With the trains so regular now a lot of people go travelling for business and it could bring you in a good income. What do you think?"

"Me?" Dilys said. "Run a business? D'you really think I could?" She stared at them, her eyes suddenly alight in her pale, worn face. "Why, it'd be like a dream. Living in a house that's not forever smothered in coal dust, cooking good food – and the little ones giving me a hand instead of going down the mine, perhaps even getting a bit of schooling… But there'd be accounts and such to keep – I don't know a thing about all that."

"You can learn," Bron said stoutly. "You can come to London and learn beside me, while Megan stays here to look after the family. Arthur's going to make enquiries straight away about a suitable house, and they can move in and get everything ready. You'll be a businesswoman in no time at all."

"Me!" Dilys said wonderingly. "Me, running my own business. A clean business, in a clean house, with enough food to put in the children's bellies every day. I can hardly believe it."

Megan smiled at her mother. She moved closer and took her hand, feeling its thinness and the roughness of the skin. She looked around at her grandmother and the kind face of Arthur Coleman.

"It's true," she said. "It's all true. Everything's going to be all right now, Mam, you'll see."

And she thought back over the past year and felt a deep sense of gratitude for all that had happened. For Mrs Gower at the big house, who had given her the money to go to London. For Sally and Etty, who had been such good friends. For the baker and his wife – for Aggie Crowther who had taken her in, even if she had treated her like a slave. And for Tom.

"I'll see you again soon," he'd told her as they'd said goodbye at Paddington Station. "I'm not letting you go out of my life, Meggie. We'll be together again."

Tom. The best friend she had ever had. She felt in her pocket and closed her fingers around the little wooden doll he had given her at the ice fair.

Everything would be all right, now.

Epilogue

Spring came slowly after that terrible winter, but nothing could hold it back for ever. The daffodils opened their buds in the valleys of Wales, and the trees put out tender green leaves. The ice melted from the mountain streams and the sun was warm as it shone from a clear blue sky.

With her mother away in London, Megan had plenty to keep her busy. Owen was still working in the pit and the other children earning whatever they could, but Arthur had found a house suitable for a hostelry and they had moved out of the hovel to live there. It had been an ironmaster's house and had been empty for a while, and Megan found plenty of cleaning to do to get it ready for her mother's new business.

Sometimes of an evening, when the little ones were in bed, she would shut the door behind her and stroll up the mountain path, away from the gritty air of the valley. She would sit on a rock, watch the sunset and think of Tom, reading and re-reading his letters.

"It seems lonely in London without you," he wrote. "I keep seeing you in the streets, and sometimes I think my heart will jump right out of me, like a dog going to its owner. I want to be near you. I want to know you're here, close to me."

"I miss you too," Megan wrote back. "I've got my little doll where I can see it, and I never look at it without remembering the day we went to the ice fair. I keep remembering the night of the bread riot and the way you rescued me from Peg."

She was sad to read one day that Etty had died. Bron had taken her in and looked after her, giving her the rest and the good food and comfort she needed, but it was too late to save the frail, damaged body and one night she fell asleep and did not wake again.

At last the day came when Dilys was to return from London. Megan went to the station to meet her. Eagerly, she scanned the carriages for the familiar face of her mother. Then she stared.

"Tom!"

"Megan!" He leapt down from the train before it had properly stopped and caught her in his arms. "What do you think of this? I nearly wrote to tell you I was coming – but I wanted it to be a surprise. I wanted to see your face."

"Oh Tom!" She was almost crying. "What are you doing here? How long can you stay?"

Dilys stepped down from the train to join them. Her face was plumper and she looked happy and confident. She smiled at Megan.

"There you are, *cariad*. It's good to see you again. And what do you think of my new baker?"

"Your *baker*?" Megan asked, bewildered. "But –

you don't mean – *Tom*?"

"Indeed I do," Dilys said, laughing. "Tom's agreed to come and set up as a baker for me. His father's said he can spare him for a year at least, and then Tom's to decide whether he wants to stay here or go back to London."

"I'm not leaving you behind again, Meggie," Tom said to her in a low voice. "If I go back to London, it'll be with you – or we'll both stop here in the valley. I've been really miserable without you, and I'm not letting you out of my sight again. All right?"

"Oh, yes, Tom," Megan said, hugging his arm. "That's all right. That's *very* all right."

"And I'm 'ere too!" Megan turned from Tom's arms and saw Sally laughing at her from Dilys's other side. "I'm goin' to be a waitress and chambermaid and jack of all trades, that's me. I'm fed up with London – thought it was time I saw a bit of the world."

"Oh Sally! Oh, it's so good to see you all!" Megan felt as if she wanted to hug them all at once. Instead, she took it in turns, finishing with Tom again, and she clung to his arm as they walked through the streets towards Dilys's new home, where the rest of the family was waiting.

It was a year since her father had died – a year of misery and fear. But now they could look forward to a brighter future. They were all together at last, all the people she loved best in the world. And as she hugged Tom's arm against her, Megan knew that the year of misery was over.

Historical Note

The Victorian age was hard for many people. Wages were low, housing was poor and even those who had regular jobs lived very harsh lives. There was no welfare state to look after those who had no job or home, only a small amount of poor relief or the workhouse. Thousands of people, many of them children, lived on the streets in big cities such as London.

1860–61 was one of the worst winters known. It was nearly the end of a period called the Little Ice Age, and it was so cold that on the Serpentine, London's famous lake in Hyde Park, there was a thirty-three-centimetre-deep layer of ice – solid enough to turn it into a fairground, with ice-skating competitions, ice-dancing, concerts and firework displays. Sometimes there would be as many as 50,000 people on the ice, as well as fashionable carriages, refreshment tents, charcoal braziers and several hundred stalls selling hot chestnuts to the crowds. There may still be very old people alive today who can remember their parents or grandparents telling them about this wonderful carnival on ice.

But there wasn't much pleasure for those who had

no homes, or who had lost their jobs because of the freezing cold. For them, the bitter weather meant no money to buy food or fuel. Thousands faced death.

Clergymen, ragged schools and charities all tried to help, but there were so many people in need that they could not cope with them all. Huge crowds of starving people gathered each day at the workhouse, begging for bread. But there wasn't enough to go round.

By the middle of January, the poor were so desperate that they began to attack the bakers' shops and then became more violent and attacked any shop that sold food. Even the mounted police couldn't control the mobs.

Today everyone is entitled to help from the state, yet in some ways, London was not so different then from what it is now. There are still homeless people on the streets and a lot of them are young people who, like Megan, have gone to seek a better life. There are still dangers threatening such youngsters, and Peg and Aggie still have their modern counterparts who are ready to take advantage of them.